WILD RUNAWAY

WILD HEART MOUNTAIN: WILD RIDERS MC
BOOK THREE

SADIE KING

WILD RIDERS MC

AN INTRODUCTION

Welcome to Wild Heart Mountain home of the Wild Riders MC.

If you love damaged heroes and curvy girl romance, then you'll love the Wild Riders MC.

This group of ex-military bikers fall hard and fall fast when they encounter the curvy women who heal their hearts.

Expect forbidden love, age gap, forced proximity, fake relationships, single dads, single moms and off-limits love with protective heroes who will do anything for the women they love.

Spend some time with Wild Heart Mountain's Wild Riders MC, the MC that's all heart.

Let me introduce you to the members…

Ex-military buddies **Raiden, Quentin and Travis** formed the Wild Riders MC when they got out of the military and wanted to create a place for veterans who love to ride.

They set up their headquarters in a compound on the side of Wild Heart Mountain.

Travis, whose road name is Hops, runs the Wild Taste Bar and Restaurant, and secretly crushes on his best friend's sister.

Quentin, also known as Barrels, runs the award-winning Wild Taste Brewery located out the back of the restaurant. He was a First Class Sargent in the army and you wouldn't want to cross him. Especially where his little sister is concerned...

Colter, or Vintage, is a motorbike mechanic and runs the bike shop. He collects old bikes and loves all things vintage especially the bubbly Danni and her 1950's curves.

Calvin also known as Badge, is the local Sheriff and his uptight views that are shaped by loss.

Joseph, or Lone Star is a recluse whose military experiences have given him a distaste for humanity.

Grant goes by Snips. He's the local barber and a single dad.

Arlo earns the road name Prince because of his charming and personable nature. He loves getting under the skin of Maggie, the shy pastry chef.

Davis begins the series as a prospect. Younger than most of the other men, he came out of the military with diminished hearing. His hearing aids keeps make him shy with women and he keeps himself hidden away.

Luke becomes a prospect after Raiden finds him drinking himself to oblivion in a strip joint. A wheelchair user since he lost both his legs in Afghanistan, Luke finds new purpose with the MC, but can he find love?

Specs would rather read a book than talk to anyone.

Bit Rate is a grumpy single dad widower in need of a nanny.

Judge is a military lawyer and always does the right thing until he meets the curvy woman who makes him question his world view.

Marcus goes by Wood because his family own the local sawmill and it's his medium of choice. He channels his PTSD into his art, creating sculptures that attract the attention of an arts journalist from the city.

On the other side of Wild Heart Mountain is a town called Hope and nestled in the hills is the Emerald Heart Resort. During the summer, it's a popular destination for tourists and in winter, they come for the ski season. Perfect for a snowed in romance...

Stay awhile in Wild Heart Mountain and explore the other series set here.

Wild Heart Mountain: Military Heroes
Wild Heart Mountain: Mountain Heroes
Temptation
A Runaway Bride for Christmas
A Secret Baby for Christmas

WILD RUNAWAY

A single mom in danger and the ex-military biker who becomes her protector...

I found her on the doorstep with a baby in her arms.

A woman on the run, as damaged as I am.

We each have our demons from the past. Mine are internal and harder to fight, remnants from my days in the military. But I can take on Trish's demons.

When her ex comes to claim her, he doesn't expect to find an entire MC club of hardened ex-military mountain men fighting her corner.

Because I'll do anything to protect my wild runaway.

Wild Runaway is a single mom in danger, MC-lite romance featuring an ex-military protector hero and the curvy woman who runs away with his heart.

www.authorsadieking.com

CONTENT ADVISORY

Dear Reader,

Joseph and Trish's story deals with issues of domestic abuse off the page. If you find this upsetting then please proceed with caution.

Rest assured, they get the HEA they deserve and Trish finds safety in the arms of her true protector hero.

-Sadie

1
JOSEPH

The half a deer carcass in the back of the pickup bumps up and down as I drive over the uneven surface of the mountain road. I watch it in the rearview mirror, wondering if I should have strapped it down better or if it'll jump right out of the crate.

It's a fresh kill from today, and I'm making good on my promise to give a shank to Kobe. He's got a baby on the way, and I don't mind sharing my meat with others on the mountain who need it.

The private gravel road that leads to Kobe and Hailey's cabin is lined with tall pine trees and scraggly bushes that scrape against the pickup as I turn in.

The driveway opens up to the front of their classic log cabin, and as I pull up out front, I note that Kobe's pickup isn't here. I guess I should have called ahead, but I like doing things the old-fashioned way. I grew up in the mountains, and if you wanted to visit your neighbor, and by neighbor I mean any other mountain dweller, you just turned up.

As I cut the engine, I realize there's someone sitting on the front steps.

A woman is hunched over on the stairs that lead down from the front porch. She's clutching something close to her chest, and her brown eyes are wide and staring. She's as frightened as a deer in the forest, and the way she's poised, with a hand on the banister and one foot on the bottom steps, ready to leap up at any moment, she's just as flighty.

We stare at each other, her breathing hard, clearly wondering if she should make a dash for it, and me paralyzed by the vision before me. Because she is a vision. Sunlight dances off her long golden hair as it cascades over her shoulders. She's got pale, smooth skin and full, youthful lips. Hell, she's at least ten years younger than me, but there's something in the set of her eyes, a wariness that makes her look older.

I don't know who she is or why she's here, but my instinct tells me any sudden movement could scare her off.

Instead of getting out of the car, I wind the window down and we stare at each other. My mouth goes dry as I drink her in. I've never seen anyone so beautiful, and I've got no clue what to say to her.

I clear my throat, and she startles. Christ, the woman's jumpier than a newborn fawn.

"Are you a friend of Hailey's?"

I take a guess that she's here for Kobe's wife. They look about the same age, and I figure if I drop Hailey's name she'll realize I'm not a stranger.

The woman pulls her eyebrows together and adjusts whatever it is she's clutching to her chest.

"Who are you?"

Her voice is bold, and I like that. She may be trembling like a deer, but she's putting on a show of bravado.

"Name's Joseph. I served with Kobe."

She relaxes a little. Being ex-military has that effect on people. They feel they can trust you because you served their country. But the things I saw people doing to each other over there made me lose all hope in humanity. It's why I live deep in the mountains, why I only come out for my motorcycle club or to run errands like this.

The rest of humanity can go to hell. I've seen too much madness. I've seen what people can do to each other, and I'd rather keep my own company with the animals of the forest.

If it weren't for the Wild Riders MC, I'd never leave my patch of forest at all. I hunt or grow most of the food I need and live off the grid with my own set-up. There's not much I need people for. But Kobe was a brother in arms, and we hunt together sometimes.

"Do you know where Kobe and Hailey are?" the woman asks without telling me her name.

She's afraid of something or someone, I'd bet my best gun on it. A wave of protectiveness hits me so suddenly that I sit back in my seat. I don't know this woman, but I want to keep her safe from whatever she's scared of. I just need her to trust me.

"Dunno. I stopped by to drop some meat off."

Her shoulders sag, and the thing she's holding to her chest moves. She glances down at it and read-justs herself. She's got something alive there, I'm sure. Maybe a puppy or something she found in the woods.

"You been waiting long?"

She stares at me long and hard, and I get the feeling she's assessing me. I tug on my beard, not sure how I measure up. A grizzled mountain man with half a deer in the back of his pickup. If I'd known I was going to meet this beauty today, I would have trimmed my beard and put my best flannel on.

Still, something must work in my favor, because she lets out a long breath and relaxes a little.

"I've been waiting for a few hours."

As she says it, a breeze rustles the surrounding trees, and whatever adrenaline she had warming her veins when I showed up dissipates, because she shivers and hunches over.

As she shivers, the bundle in her arms wriggles again and a thin cry pierces the air. Her attention snaps to the bundle and she bounces it up and down, making shushing noises.

Realization hits me.

"You've got a baby?"

She turns away and pulls the thing closer as if I'm going to jump out and snatch it. My mind's working overtime wondering what the hell this young woman is doing sitting out in the cold with a baby for hours on end in nothing but a thin coat.

I glance around the area in case I've missed something, but there's no sign of a car. No indication of how she got here or what she's doing here. But she's cold and she's got a crying baby. She needs my help.

I open the cab to the pickup and she stands up

and backs onto the deck, the flighty look coming into her eyes.

I hold my hands up.

"I'm not gonna hurt you. The wind's picking up and you look cold."

She bounces the baby and stares at me but doesn't respond. Tiny cries echo around the forest, and the sound is so alien to me it makes me wince. I turn away before she can see and get the blanket from the back.

I want to wrap it around her myself, take care of her so she can take care of her baby. But I sense any movement might scare her take off. And it's important to me that I keep talking to her.

I walk to the bottom of the stairs and hold the blanket up. She snatches it off me and retreats to the deck. Ignoring herself, she wraps it around the child, tucking it around the small body and leaving half of it trailing down her hip.

There's a small backpack leaning against the front door, but she doesn't appear to have anything else with her. I wonder again who she is and what she's doing here and why I feel so damn protective of her.

I can't leave her here on her own, especially with a baby.

"You want to call them and see if you can find out when they're coming home?"

She nods. "My phone's out of battery. I left in a hurry…" She snaps her mouth shut as if she's said too much.

I want to admonish her for venturing into the mountains on her own with only a light jacket and no means of communication. But she's obviously not from around here and doesn't know how dangerous the mountain can be. She probably doesn't even have bear spray.

I slide my phone out of my pocket.

"I don't have Hailey's number, but you can call Kobe."

I hold out the phone, and she takes it with her free arm. I'm rewarded with a small smile.

"Thank you."

I can hear the tone indicating that the call's not connecting. Wherever Kobe is he hasn't got signal, which isn't unusual. Parts of the mountain are blissfully still dark spots.

She hands back the phone, and her eyebrows are knit together with worry. The baby scrunches up its face and lets out a bellow.

"She's hungry."

There's a desperate tone to her voice, and I guess she hasn't got any food with her.

"I've got deer in the back if she wants some?"

It's meant to be a joke, even I know you don't feed raw meat to a baby, but the woman frowns. "She's not on solids yet. I've got milk in my bag but no way to heat it."

She sticks her chin out, daring me to call her a bad mother. Hell, I'm not judging. I don't know her circumstances, but I guess she wouldn't be out here in the cold with an infant if there wasn't a damn good reason for it.

"I can call some people and see if anyone knows where Kobe and Hailey are."

She tugs on her lower lip and looks away. She's worried about something. Maybe she doesn't want anyone to know she's here.

"I'll call Symon, the ranger. He knows the comings and goings of everyone on this mountain, and he's discreet."

She looks back at me and nods.

I bring up Symon's number as she jiggles the baby on her hip.

"Who will I say is looking for them?"

She bits her lip again, leaving imprints from her teeth. She worries it a lot, and I long to run my thumb over the puckered skin and smooth it out.

"Trish," she finally says. "I'm Hailey's sister."

"Trish." I like the sound of her name. It's fierce like she is. "I'll call the ranger."

I make the call to Symon, but no one picks up. I leave him a quick message without mentioning Trish.

Next, I call the Wild Taste Bar and Restaurant. It's where the HQ for the Wild Riders MC is based. Kobe and Hailey often come over for lunch or a drink. Every man in the MC is ex-military, and Kobe knows a fair few of us. He's social for a mountain man and likes to keep in touch, but we all know he's checking in on us. Making sure no one falls over the edge of the precipice that so many of us came back tottering along.

Kendra picks up the phone. She's Barrel's sister and Hops's old lady. That caused a huge stir and nearly got Hops banished from the club, but luckily they sorted out their differences.

"Are Kobe and Hailey up there?"

Kendra checks the restaurant, but no one's seen them. Hops is speaking in the background, and Kendra must hand the phone across to him.

"They're away for the weekend. Went to the coast."

That will explain the phone. They've probably got a remote spot where there's no signal. Having some time together before the baby arrives.

"I went up there to give Kobe some deer meat and found a girl on their doorstep. Says she's Hailey's sister."

Trish gives me a worried look, but I can trust my MC brothers. They won't breathe a word.

"Is she okay?" Kendra asks.

I glance at Trish, and she's cradling the baby. The shushing seems to have worked, but all of a sudden the infant lifts its tiny pink head and gives an almighty wail.

"Is that a baby?" asks Hops.

The pink mouth is contorted into an angry cry that's so loud it's scaring the birds away.

"Yup, she's got a baby with her."

Trish bounces the infant on her shoulder as she paces the porch. Tiny fingers grasp at her hair, and she looks down at the pink scrunched up face with love. Even though the thing is screaming at her, even though it's cold and windy and I just felt the first drops of rain, all I see emanating from her is love.

A bolt of realization shoots through my veins. I want that love trained on me.

The thought is so strong it makes me stagger. I don't know anything about this curvy beauty, but she's vulnerable out here. Her and the baby, they need me. My heart does a little flip, and my chest swells with new purpose.

Whatever this woman is running from, whatever she and her baby need, I will provide. A surge of protectiveness rushes through me, and I know I'll do whatever it takes to keep Trish and her baby safe.

Kendra's saying something on the other end of the line, asking if they need help, but I barely hear her. I know my purpose; I know what I need to do.

"She's fine," I say. "I'll take care of it."

I hang up the phone and slide it back in my pocket. I've never been around a baby, and it's been years since I was with a woman. But I'll do whatever I need to do to take care of these two.

2

TRISH

I keep my face turned down, focusing on the tiny bundle in my arms. It's been over five hours since Rose had her last bottle. The train took me to the town of Hope, and I stopped at a cafe where they let me heat up a bottle for her even though I didn't buy anything.

My tummy rumbled at the cakes and sticky pastries in the cabinet, but I couldn't risk spending any money unnecessarily.

When I left home this morning, I only had time to grab the backpack I kept stashed in the bottom of Rose's diaper drawer, the one place Ian would never go.

The cafe let me use their phone to call Hailey, but it didn't connect. I found the only taxi in town and used the last of my money to take it up the mountain. My cash didn't quite cover the fair and I said I'd walk the rest of the way, but the kind man insisted on driving me all the way.

When I took the cash from what Ian thinks is his secret stash this morning, I thought there would be more, but it barely covered the cost of getting here. I'm at the mercy of my sister and strangers, and that terrifies me.

I couldn't choose the time of my leaving, so it wasn't a surprise that Hailey and Kobe weren't in. But it was five hours waiting on their doorstep until the giant man in the mud-splattered pickup turned up.

I watch Joseph out of the corner of my eye as he speaks on the phone. He's the biggest man I've ever seen, even bigger than my brother-in-law, Kobe. Joseph has a full rugged beard and the brightest blue eyes I've ever seen. They seem out of place in his weathered, tanned face. Too bright and blue for a mountain man.

He ends the call and slides the phone into his pocket.

"They've gone away for a few days."

The words make my heart sink and I sag to the ground, feeling the weight of what I've done.

Hailey was my last chance, the only place I could turn. I never expected she wouldn't be here when I turned up. But I can't go back, and not just because I don't have the funds. I'd rather camp out in the woods than go back to Ian.

Tears threaten my eyes and I blink them back quickly, but not before Joseph sees.

"Hey." His voice is a gentle rumble and soothes a deep part of my soul. "You can shelter at my place until they get back."

I jerk my head up. He seems nice and he's been kind, but I just met this stranger.

"We're fine."

He keeps his eyes on me, not convinced.

"You don't know me, Trish, but you need shelter and that baby needs milk. You can heat the bottle in my kitchen and do what you need to do to look after that baby, and I'll stay out in the pickup if that makes you feel better."

It does. Kind of. But also a little disappointed. I might not know this mountain giant, but the way he looks at me makes my body come alive in a way I haven't felt in a long time. I push the thought away. I have to do what's best for my daughter.

A gust of wind whips my hair around my face, and a drop of rain hits my cheek. I look up at the darkening sky. Rose howls, and I snap my gaze back to her. The way her face puckers with hunger makes my heart hurt. Whatever I do, I need to do something soon.

"I don't have much choice."

Joseph stares at me. "You do have a choice," he says slowly. "I can drive you somewhere, anywhere you want to go, or back to wherever you came from."

I shudder, and he notices.

"Or to a hotel if you prefer."

I lower my eyes, not wanting him to see the shame that heats my face. I don't have any money. I'm completely reliant on the kindness of this stranger.

I look at Joseph long and hard, mentally running through the things I know about him. He's a friend of Kobe's, and Kobe doesn't suffer fools, so he must be a decent guy. He's ex-military, but for the first time I notice what he's wearing over his faded flannel shirt: a motorcycle club jacket with a patch.

"You're in an MC?"

My danger sense goes up a notch, and I pull Rose close.

"The Wild Riders. We're ex-military guys who love to ride. That's all. No funny business, no hassle."

Where I come from, an MC means bad news. They ride around on their big bikes intimidating the locals and getting in trouble with the law. But again, what choice do I have?

"Okay," I say, hoping like hell I don't regret it.

I go to grab my bag from the porch, but he gets there first. As I straighten up our arms brush, and a spark of heat jumps from his body to mine. I gasp, and my eyes meet his. From this close up, I see all the shades of blue in their depths. There are lines around his eyes, a weariness that tells of hurt.

Joseph may be kind and genuine, but there's pain in his past too. I'm sure of it. For some strange reason I find that comforting, seeing my pain reflected in him.

Then he smiles and his eyes sparkle, and the moment passes.

He takes my bag and opens the pickup's back door. "Come on. Let's get your baby some milk."

3
JOSEPH

*M*y gaze slides to the rearview mirror and Trish sitting in the backseat.

Blonde hair falls over her face as she gazes down at her baby. The motion of the pickup seems to have lulled it to sleep, and a smile spreads over Trish's lips as she watches her daughter.

There's something warming in the way she's looking at the baby that I can't look away from. She's the picture of motherhood, despite the dark shadows under her eyes and unwashed hair. Her expression is serene when she watches her daughter.

Trish must feel my gaze on her, because she glances up and our eyes meet. I look away quickly, but not before I see the haunted expression in her eyes. She may appear serene when she watches her daughter, but there's a restless energy about her at other times. She's running from something, but I don't know what.

I take the drive easy, aware of my precious cargo in the back seat. Trish's nose twitched when she got in next to the deer, but she had the good grace not to say anything about her bloody companion.

There's not a lot I can do about the deer carcass riding alongside her. I don't know how long Kobe will be away, so I didn't want to leave it. I'll stick it in the deep freeze and give it to them when they get back.

We arrive at my cabin as the sky is turning grey with dusk. Trish bites her lip when she sees my ramshackle cabin in the woods. It's not a nicely constructed cabin like Kobe's. My cabin was put together with my own two hands. I felled the trees, cleared the small area of land, and built it myself while living in a temporary shelter nearby.

Solar panels cover the roof, catching the rays that come through the clearing, and water comes from a well I dug in the ground.

It's one bedroom, all this single man has needed, until now.

By the time we get out of the car, the baby's crying again. This time it's angry cries, and even I can tell the poor little thing is hungry.

"What do you need?" I ask Trish as soon as we get

inside. I dump her bag in the entryway and switch on the lights for the kitchen.

The cabin is an open plan with the kitchen on the right and the living room on the left. A small table sits against the wall and there are two steps that lead to the bedroom and the bathroom.

"Hot water to heat the bottle or a microwave if you have it."

I'm not big on appliances, so I get the kettle boiling for the water. Trish crouches next to her bag and attempts to open it with one hand while cradling the baby. I haven't seen her put the thing down, and I wonder if she ever does.

"Let me help."

I crouch down to open the bag for her, but instead she holds the baby toward me. Its tiny mouth is wide open, and the noise emanating from it makes my ears bleed.

Trish gives me a reassuring smile. "Can you take her while I fix the bottle? It'll be quicker."

I'm touched that she trusts me enough to hold the infant, but I'm not sure she should. I've never held a baby before. I'm more used to wielding axes and hunting rifles, not tiny babies who wiggle and cry.

"You'll be fine. Just hold her like you would a football."

I take the infant uncertainly, and I must look terrified because Trish laughs. For a moment, the haunted expression leaves her eyes and they sparkle like sun reflecting on a mountain lake. Then she turns her attention to getting the things she needs from her bag.

I hold the baby in front of me, not sure what to do. She's staring at her momma and wiggling like a hare caught in a trap. There's an acrid stench coming from under the blanket that must mean she needs a diaper change.

I glance at Trish, but she's busy in the kitchen mixing formula into a bottle. I'm on my own.

"Hey," I say to the baby.

She looks startled by my voice and her head turns to look at me, the crying stopping for a moment.

Warmth spreads in my chest. I made the baby stop crying. We stare at each other, her curious blue eyes looking at me expectantly. I don't know what to do. I'm not much of a talker at the best of times, and I know fuck all about talking to a baby.

When I don't say anything, her eyes scrunch up and her mouth opens.

"Hey," I say quickly. I guess my voice is lower and gruffer than what she's used to, because she stares at me again.

Her little hand reaches out and grabs my beard. She looks surprised at the texture, and her brow furrows in an adorable frown.

I don't know what to say to a baby, so I smile and introduce myself.

"I'm Joseph. Some people call me Lone Star."

Her face squeezes up, and just when I think I'm winning her over, she lets out a howl that would scare the bears from the woods.

Trish comes over and takes her off me, and it's a relief to hand her over. I can coax a wild deer out of a trap, but I've got no idea how to calm a human baby.

"Let's get you changed while your milk's warming."

She looks around the cabin, and I wonder how it looks through the eyes of a mom. There's an open fireplace with a deerskin rug on the wooden floor and a sharp-edged coffee table. On one wall is my gun rack, and on the other are floor to ceiling windows, clear glass that looks straight into the depths of the dark forest.

Nope, it's not designed for babies, and I have a pang of regret. When I built this place, it was with myself in mind. Now I wonder what it would be like to have Trish and the baby around for good.

I shake the thought out of my head. It would be

noisy and stinky if the last few minutes are anything to go by.

"Is there somewhere I can change her?"

I stare at her blankly until I realize she's talking about changing the diaper.

"The bedroom? Or the floor or the kitchen table?"

I don't know what she needs. I've never had a baby in my cabin before.

"Any flat surface will do." She slings her bag over her shoulder. "But probably not the kitchen table." Her nose crinkles up in an adorable way, and she smiles.

"You can use the bed."

She throws her bag over her shoulder and follows me into the bedroom. "I don't have a changing mat. Do you have an old towel or something I can throw down, just in case?"

I don't want to know what the just in case is. I grab a towel from the hallway closet and put it on my bed.

Trish lays the baby down, and I avert my eyes before I see something that can't be unseen.

"The bathroom's through there." I indicate the closed door as I shuffle out of the room, trying not to see the unwrapping of the diaper. "There's a bath if you want to bathe her. Or yourself."

An image of Trish naked and in my bath fills my head, and I practically run out of the bedroom. This woman's got me thinking about things I thought I was done with in my life.

I grip the kitchen counter and breathe hard, trying to control the storm of emotions inside me. How can one woman and one tiny baby make me feel so out of control?

"Get it together," I mutter to myself. She needs shelter, not a man ogling her and imagining her naked.

There's a stack of wood by the fire, and I get the fire going to warm the place up.

Trish comes out a few moments later and tests the milk, then settles with the baby on the couch to feed.

With a dry diaper and milk in her belly, the crying finally stops. A content silence settles on the cabin. It's a lovely sight, Trish feeding the baby in front of the fire, the only sounds the crackle of the flames and the baby suckling.

The silence is golden, and I release a breath I didn't know I was holding.

"Do they always cry that much?"

Trish glances up. "It's been a long day. Her routine is out of whack."

I want to ask why her day has been long and

23

what she's running from. But at that moment the baby stirs, and Trish's attention is back on her daughter.

I leave her to it while I get busy in the kitchen. Trish looks like she needs looking after just as much as the baby. And I'll be the one to take care of her.

4
TRISH

ith Rose's needs met, my anxiety eases a little. My baby girl is fed and changed, and we have shelter and a safe place to stay. It's more than we've had since she was born four months ago.

I've only known Joseph for a few short hours, but I'm starting to relax around him. A man who helps a woman and baby in need can't be all bad.

I wish I could get hold of Hailey, but hers and Kobe's phones are still out of range of any signal. With Rose fed, I realize how woefully unprepared I am. There's nowhere for her to sleep.

Joseph offers up his bed, which is so kind of him that I almost cry. But I turn away quickly and help him roll up towels to form a barrier for Rose. It's not ideal and I probably won't sleep a wink, but it will have to do until I can figure out my next move.

Joseph leaves me alone to get Rose down to sleep, and I lie on the bed with her and hold her close. The bed smells masculine, like pine and oil, and a new sensation weaves itself into my veins. What would it be like to lie in here with Joseph, to have his muscular arms wrapped around me, to feel his body pressed against mine?

I shake the thought out of my head. There's no point having indecent thoughts about my rescuer. He's just a kind man doing the decent thing.

Rose makes a contented gurgling sound, and I kiss the top of her downy head.

"I'm sorry this was a bad day, baby girl." My hand rubs circles on her back as she snuggles into my chest. "But I hope it will be worth it."

There's a knot in my stomach that has been there since this morning, but as I press Rose's tiny body close and breathe in her milky scent, the knot eases a little.

My daughter is safe, and that's all that matters. Hailey will be home soon, and then I'll figure something out for us.

Hailey always told me I could come to her anytime. That's what sisters are for. She tried to get me to leave Ian sooner, but I stupidly thought things would get better once we had the baby. They didn't. They got worse.

Rose's breathing turns heavy, and I watch her sleep for a few minutes before placing her carefully between the towels and tiptoeing out of the bedroom.

The scent of frying garlic and rosemary hits me, and my stomach gives a lurching rumble. I cross my arms over it, horrified that Joseph heard. But he doesn't say anything.

"I've made stew."

He indicates for me to sit at the small kitchen table, and I slump into the seat. With Rose asleep, the adrenaline I've been running on all day leaves my body and I'm suddenly exhausted.

Joseph puts a large bowl of stew in front of me, and I attack it hungrily.

"Thank you," I say between mouthfuls.

I don't know what the meat is, but it's rich and lean, and with all the flavors he's included it's the best meal I've ever had.

"I'll pay you back for all this." Although I'm not sure how.

He shakes his head. "No you won't."

I choke on my mouthful, wondering if he can tell I don't have a dime to my name.

"You and the little one can stay as long as you

need. Don't worry about money or any kind of payback."

He says it in a tone as if it's all decided. Like taking a stranger and her baby in are normal things to do. And maybe they are if you're a good person.

Suddenly, there's a sting of tears behind my eyes. The one person who was supposed to love me treated me like shit, yet this stranger has taken me and my child in, fed us, and given us shelter. I didn't know there was still this level of kindness in the world.

"Hell, don't cry."

Joseph reaches across the table and lays his meaty hand over mine. The warmth from him makes me sob harder.

"Sorry," I say between tears. "You've been so kind."

With his warm hand on mine, the first kind touch I've had in months, the flood gates open and I can't stop them. Everything I've been holding back for the last few months bubbles up inside me.

Joseph doesn't ask questions, which is good because I'm not ready to tell my story. Instead, he comes around to my side of the table and crouches next to my chair. His strong arms fold around me and he holds me silently as I cry, snot running into his checkered shirt.

We stay like that for a long time until my sobs dry up. I feel utterly drained when I sit back on my chair. But the knot in my stomach has lessened, and my chest feels less tight. For the first time today, I feel like I did the right thing.

Joseph trains his sparkling blue eyes on me. They're full of concern and warmth and a flash of something else. I recognize it as desire before he sits back on his haunches and looks down.

My body tingles. I'm red-eyed and puffy and covered in snot, but one look from this man has my core clenching and heat coursing through my veins.

It's been a long time since someone held me and a long time since a man looked at me with desire, no matter how fleeting. I need to get a grip.

"Thank you, Joseph. I mean it. We had nowhere else to go today."

He lifts his hand, and I think he's going to touch my face, but instead he does this awkward pat on my head.

"I'll look after you, Trish. You and the baby. You have nothing to worry about again."

His words are confusing. The tone sounds final, like he'll always look after me and Rose, but that's ridiculous. He must just mean while we're here.

He stands back on his feet and clears the bowls away.

I try to help with the washing up, but Joseph won't let me. Instead, he runs a bath for me and insists I bathe and get to sleep. I don't fight it; the day has left me exhausted, and I can barely keep my eyes open.

"I'll sleep in the pickup so you have nothing to worry about," he says.

I shake my head. "You don't need to do that. It's bad enough that we've taken your bed. At least sleep on the couch."

I barely know him, but I feel I can trust Joseph. More than that, as I soak in his giant bathtub, my thoughts go to the feel of his arms around me, how he smelled like pine and rosemary, the way my heartbeat quickened when he hugged me, and those sparkling blue intense eyes.

I shake the thoughts out of my head. He's the first man who's been kind. That's all it is. He'd do the same for anyone, and if there's one lesson I should have learned by now, it's not to get carried away when a man shows you kindness. It doesn't last.

But he's different.

My heart whispers things to me that I'm not ready to hear.

I drain the bath and snuggle next to Rose. She seems safe enough in her makeshift towel crib, and I'm soon fast asleep.

5
JOSEPH

*M*ornings are my favorite time in the cabin. With a steaming coffee, I sit out on the porch listening to the bird chatter, the wind rustling the leaves, and the wildlife shuffling through the undergrowth.

But the morning after Trish and the baby crash into my world is different.

It's before dawn when the cries reach my ears. They're muffled, coming from the bedroom, but they permeate the stillness of the cabin.

I pad to the bedroom door and hear Trish making shushing noises. The baby's probably hungry and needs a bottle.

I knock gently and push the door open, intending to let Trish know I'm awake and she can use the kitchen to heat the bottle. But the words die on my lips.

She's wearing one of my t-shirts, which hangs almost to her knees and hugs her curvy figure. One side is snagged on Rose's blanket and it pulls upward, exposing a thick creamy thigh. My mouth goes dry as I think about sliding my hand up the t-shirt and discovering what's at the top of her luscious thighs. I drag my gaze away, but my dirty thoughts follow as I glimpse her tits pushed up against the t-shirt. She's braless, and the shape of her nipple presses against the cotton.

My dick stirs to life, and I've barely got my eyes open but I'm already imagining all sorts of dirty things I want to do to her.

I turn away, intending to get out of here before Trish sees the tenting in my track pants. She's pacing the room jiggling Rose on her hip, but before I can retreat, she sees me.

"Sorry we woke you."

I shake my head. "Don't matter." I'm an early riser anyway. "She need milk?"

Trish nods and follows me to the kitchen. I focus on what she and the baby need, trying to calm my racing male blood. I thought I was done with women, but twelve hours with this one in my cabin and my body's behaving like I'm a teenager.

Trish holds Rose while I get the formula ready, trying to remember what I saw her do yesterday. The tin of formula is light when I pick it up, and I have to tip it sideways to get to the powder at the bottom. I don't know if she's got any more in her bag, but this won't last another day.

While the bottle warms, Trish changes Rose and I make the coffee. Then we all sit out on the porch, the baby wrapped in a blanket as she sucks on her bottle.

As soon as Rose gets the teat of the bottle in her mouth, the crying finally stops. The silence is golden and we sit without talking, listening to the birdsong and the sound of the forest waking up.

"It's peaceful out here." Trish lets out a long sigh.

I take a sip of coffee and lean back in my chair.

"Yup."

The porch is positioned to face a clearing where the sun rises every morning. The pale rays warm my face and I close my eyes, enjoying the sounds of the baby suckling as Trish rocks her chair back and forth. I got the rocking chairs because I like the motion, but they're perfect for nursing babies.

A vision springs into my head, Trish and the baby here every morning by my side, rocking gently on the porch as we watch the sunrise.

A smile creeps over my face. I've never contemplated being with anyone until now, let alone a woman and a baby. But I like having Trish and Rose here. It's soothing to watch her with the baby in a way that speaks to my damaged soul.

When I came back from the military, I didn't want to be around people. I'd seen the worst of humanity, but Trish is showing me the best. The love of a mother and the fierce protectiveness toward her young.

I didn't have any family when I got out of the military and Kobe told me about the Wild Riders MC, a motorcycle club of ex-servicemen. I've always loved to ride and I grew up in the mountains of the west, but there was nothing left for me back home. So I came here to see what it was about.

I like my quiet secluded life in the forest, but once a week I head down the mountain for the MC meetings and take part in any charity runs they're doing. I've helped my brothers build their own cabins, and I supply meat to the restaurant and to anyone who needs it.

Out here, I don't need much. I live off the land and off my military pension. I hunt and trap and sell meat and hides to the surrounding towns.

It's a good life. It's a single man's life. But now, for the first time, I want to share it with someone else. The thought both pleases and terrifies me. I'm an old man compared to Trish. I'm thirty-six, old and damaged. I have nightmares, haunted by what I saw humans do to each other. I don't like loud noises or being around people.

I stand up abruptly, not wanting to think about my failings. The best I can do is make Trish and the baby comfortable.

"I'm going for a supply run in town. What do you need?"

She hesitates, and I'm not sure if it's because of a reluctance to ask for help or if she doesn't have any money.

"I'll put it on my store account, so you don't have to pay me yet."

She doesn't have to pay me ever, but she's too proud to take charity. I've seen that before with people who need help.

"Umm." She bites her lower lip, and I wonder what's got her so troubled. I wish I could take her troubles away and make her smile and laugh like a young woman should.

"I need diapers and formula."

She looks away, and I'm sure there's more she needs, but I don't want to embarrass her. I'll pick up some baby stuff and hope it's right.

"Help yourself to anything in the cabin."

I figure getting out of the way and giving her time to get used to the place will help her relax. I head down the porch and turn around at the bottom step.

"And if you go walking in the forest, take some bear spray."

Her mouth pops open, and she pulls Rose to her chest as her eyes dart to the forest.

"Stick near the cabin and you'll be fine."

She doesn't look reassured, and I make a mental note to give her a lesson on basic mountain safety when I get back.

I chuckle to myself as I get into the pickup. This small town girl doesn't know a thing about the mountains, and I can't wait to teach her.

A few hours later, I'm at the general store in Wild. It's easy enough to get diapers here and formula, but I'll have to go across the mountain to Hope to get the other things I need.

Larry, who runs the store, looks at me suspiciously when I put the diapers down on the counter. But I don't say anything. It's none of his damn business, and I don't want to let the whole town know about Trish.

There's a baby store in Hope, and I browse the aisles trying to figure out what Rose needs. There are all in one outfits and cute animal t-shirts and tiny little dresses. I forgot to ask how old Rose is, but if human babies don't wean until six months, she must be younger than that. I pick up a cute onesie with a smiling giraffe and another with a fox. I stay away from the laughing bear; I don't want her to think bears are approachable.

Geez, if any of the guys were here they'd give me shit. But I already feel like a protective dad towards this baby.

There are a bunch of baby toys and I rifle through them, trying to find one that isn't a choking hazard. I settle on a colorful caterpillar and a wind-up car that will work well on my wooden floors.

I'm guessing Trish doesn't have a lot of baby clothes in that little bag of hers, so I throw in a couple of singlets and a baby changing mat. I find a travel crib and a baby sling. I've noticed Rose doesn't like to be put down, and this way she can stay close to her momma while Trish keeps her hands free.

I take it all to the counter and scowl when I recognize Trudy. The last time I saw Trudy was when I helped install a ramp at their house after her son had an injury and needed assistance. She'd spent the entire time telling me and the boys all the gossip on the mountain, as if we care who's seeing who and who's newly divorced and whose daughter is off to college.

"Hello Joseph." She eyes the baby stuff I put on the counter. "You got some news you want to tell me?"

Her eyes light up, eager for the gossip.

The last thing I want to do is get into a conversation about Trish. Trudy's a decent woman, but I know how town gossip works. It spreads quicker than wildfire around these mountains.

"Got a friend staying for a few days."

She wants to ask more, but I cut her off with a question about washing instructions on the baby clothes.

While she's talking, I pay up and get out of there as soon as she hands me my bags. Her curious look follows me out of the shop.

I'm walking back to the pickup when a glint of bronze in a shop window catches my eye. I stop in front of a boutique jewelry shop and stare at the clip in the window display. Trish's hair always slips over her shoulder, and a clip would help her keep it out of the way. And she'd look damn good with her hair half clipped back.

I stop into the shop, smiling to myself as I imagine her face when I give it to her.

6

TRISH

*W*ith the peace and quiet of the cabin, the knot in my stomach unwinds as the morning goes on. I give Rose tummy time on the rug, and she giggles as I pull funny faces at her.

We go for a walk outside but not too far from the cabin. Joseph freaked me out when he talked about bears.

There's a vegetable garden surrounded by chicken wire and a greenhouse with the last of the season's tomatoes. I pull out a few weeds and pick a shiny red tomato to have with lunch.

Rose gets restless, so I bring her in for another bottle and change her into the last diaper. It reminds me how lucky we are to have found Joseph. If he hadn't have shown up at Hailey's, I don't know what

I would have done. And if I didn't have Hailey to run to in the first place...

I shudder at the thought and pull Rose close to my chest.

She gurgles happily, and I walk her around the cabin until she falls asleep. It's usually the only way she can get to sleep, resting on me. Maybe she tuned in to the turmoil that was going on in the trailer where we came from. But for whatever reason, she won't sleep unless she's pressed up against me.

I walk around the cabin, rhythmically pacing until her breathing gets heavy. Once I know she's asleep, I slow down and peer at the photos on the cabin walls.

There's a group of men in front of big motorbikes like the one I noticed parked in a shed behind the cabin. They're all wearing the same leather jackets that Joseph has, but for a motorcycle club, they look friendlier than I would have imagined. I find Joseph near the back. He's the only one not smiling. His blue eyes stare intently at the camera.

Another photo shows him in his military uniform, standing tall with a group of men. He looks haunted, his gaze looking down, unable to meet the eye of the camera.

It makes me wonder why he left the military and how he ended up here. There's a lot I don't know about Joseph, only that he's kind and I feel safe in his presence. And for now, that's enough.

My arm aches, and I risk putting Rose down. I ease her between the towels of the makeshift baby bed, holding my breath as I lower her onto the bedding. She stirs but doesn't wake up. Relieved, I tip-toe out of the room but leave the door open so I'll hear her as soon as she wakes.

I make myself another cup of coffee and a tomato and cheese sandwich and eat them with my feet tucked under me on the couch. I try Hailey again, but the call doesn't connect. If she was going away on a big vacation, she would have told me, so it's likely this trip is only a weekend break and she'll be back tomorrow.

Then what?

When I left the trailer, I didn't have a plan past getting the hell away from Ian. I knew my sister would take me in, and I could figure out my next move from there. It's hard to make plans when you're fighting for survival.

I guess I'll look for a job and a place to stay. Hailey's got her own baby on the way, so I don't want to intrude on them for any longer than I have to.

If only I could stay here forever. It's so peaceful

and Joseph is so kind, not to mention the way my core tightens whenever he's nearby.

I'm pulled out of my thoughts by the sound of a car. My gut clenches, and I duck behind the couch with my heart racing. My hands grip the top of the couch, and I'm about to make a dash to the bedroom to get Rose when I recognize Joseph's pickup.

It's just Joseph returning.

Of course it is. You're safe here.

I get out from behind the couch before he can see me. My heart's still racing, and I check on Rose. The sight of her sleeping peacefully calms my nerves.

I pull the door almost shut so we don't wake her, then head outside to help Joseph with the shopping.

"I'll give you a hand."

He grunts and nods, which I'm learning means thank you. He's a man of few words, and I like that. I'm also learning that he might not talk much, but he thinks a lot. Behind his quiet demeanor, his brain is working overtime.

I grab a shopping bag from the back and gasp in surprise when I see the name on the bag.

"You went to Babyland?" It's a franchise of baby gear that's way out of my price range.

"Noticed you need a few things."

By a few things, he means two big shopping bags worth. My heart warms at his thoughtfulness.

I've never felt so cared for, and I still can't believe it's a complete stranger that's looking after me and Rose.

In the bags are baby clothes, toys, a changing mat, and a sling, which will save my sore arm. Joseph must have noticed how I'm always carrying her around, how she cries whenever I put her down. The thoughtfulness makes my eyes sting and I blink quickly, not wanting to cry again.

"This will have to do for now, until I can build you a proper one."

Joseph holds a box that says 'travel crib' on the side. It must have cost a fortune.

"You didn't have to do this." My eyes are welling up, and damn this man who makes me cry and makes my body tingle and makes me feel safe and normal for the first time in months.

"You're mine to look after Trish, you and Rose."

His words are confusing again, because Rose is not his baby and her biological father isn't interested in caring for her, so why would this stranger be? But I like the idea of being his.

"Here." He hands me a small package. "This one's for you."

I open the brown wrapping paper and turn the object over in my hand.

It's a hair comb, a polished bronze design with a

cluster of pink roses on the side. It's beautiful and not what I was expecting from a man like Joseph.

"So you can keep your hair pinned back. It gets in the way when you're feeding the little one."

Tears sting my eyes. It's the most thoughtful gift anyone's ever given me, and it's from a virtual stranger.

"Thank you." But I can't say anything else or I'll cry again.

Joseph must sense that, because he takes the clip off me. "May I?"

I love that he asked before he touched me, because I probably would have flinched if he hadn't. His rough hand slides over my silky hair, and the sensation sends sparks of heat through my body. He's so close his woodsy scent tickles my nostrils and make me want to pull him closer.

I close my eyes and inhale, loving the way he smells of fresh pine and woodsmoke, loving his touch and letting the sensations unfurling in my belly warm me up.

This is what it feels like to be touched by a man. Gentle, loving, and with care. Not rough and mean and hurtful.

I feel Joseph's touch all the way through my body to my very soul. Warmth spreads though my veins, warming up my belly and snaking right to my core.

Heat wells up between my legs, and my core throbs with need.

It's been so long since I was touched with tenderness, and a whimper escapes my lips as Joseph scoops my hair off my neck and slides the clip into place.

He's so close that his breath tickles my skin, sending tendrils of heat through my veins. His fingers pause behind my ear, and his breathing is ragged. Neither of us move and I hold my breath, not wanting this moment to end.

His fingertips brush behind my ear and trail down the soft skin of my neck. I tilt my head back, an invitation to keep going, hardly daring to breathe. He leans forward and gently presses his mouth to the delicate skin at the nape of my neck. At his touch, my body is on fire. I whimper as his mouth moves over my skin, his fingers sliding under the collar of my t-shirt.

Suddenly, he stiffens. And I freeze, remembering what's caused him to stop. I pull away, but it's too late.

"Who did this to you?"

His voice has a dangerous edge that I've not heard from him before, and it sets warning bells ringing. I scoot to the other side of the room, putting myself between him and Rose.

He must see the fear in my eyes, because his voice softens.

"I'm not going to hurt you, Trish. I would never hurt you. But somebody has."

You get so used to living with the marks on your body that you forget they're there. The fingerprints on my neck, the bruising on my collar. I run my hand over them now, embarrassed that Joseph has seen them.

"Is that why you ran?"

Joseph has his hands up in a placating gesture and he's trying to keep his voice calm, but there's rage simmering underneath.

"Yes," I whisper.

The confession feels good. I've never admitted it to anyone before. I couldn't tell Hailey, because I was too ashamed. She wouldn't have understood how you could stay with a man who does that to you.

"Do you want to tell me about it?"

I hesitate. I've never talked about the way Ian treated me. It's embarrassing to admit that the person who's supposed to love you hurts you.

But as I look at Joseph, this burly man who could snap me in two if he wanted but has shown me nothing but kindness, I feel exhausted.

I'm tired of hiding. I'm tired of pretending everything's okay. I want to tell him; I want him to see all my hidden parts. I feel I can trust him with my hurt.

Joseph takes a seat on the couch, and I join him. And once I start talking, I can't stop.

I tell him about Ian being my high school boyfriend and how it started out well, but when we moved into the trailer together things changed.

How I was going to leave him, but then I got pregnant. I thought the baby would change things, but it made them worse. He couldn't cope with the crying. He blamed me and took it out on me. That I could handle.

But the morning I left, he squeezed my neck so hard that I passed out. When I came to, he was standing over the crib with Rose in his hands. She was screaming as he held her in front of him. I grabbed her off him before he could do anything. I don't know if he would have hurt her, but I wasn't going to stick around to find out.

Ian left the trailer and I grabbed our bag, took the jar of money he had stashed away, and fled.

That's why I have hardly anything with us. I couldn't risk staying another moment in that place. I had to get her away from him.

Joseph listens in silence. A vein pulsing on his neck is the only indication that he's taking it all in and how angry it's making him to hear.

After I finish telling him my pathetic story, he takes my hand in his, his blue eyes sparking dangerously.

"I'll kill that fucking asshole."

There's a grim conviction in his voice that makes me shiver. I'm reminded of the man in uniform, the military man, the trained killer. I hate Ian, but I'd never want anyone dead.

"Don't do that," I whisper. "I got away from him. I'm never going back."

Joseph pulls me toward him, and I sink into his warmth. His touch is electric, and I want him to keep kissing me the way he was before he saw the marks on my neck.

"I promise you this, Trish. I will never let anything happen to you or Rose. You understand?"

I nod, although I'm not sure I do. How can this virtual stranger make this promise to me and the daughter that isn't his? But I can tell by the conviction in his voice that he's serious.

"You're mine to protect. And I will protect you both with my life."

It's a pledge, and a man who's sworn an oath to die for his country doesn't make promises lightly. The tightness in my stomach eases, and I lean into him.

I've got Joseph fighting in my corner. I don't understand why, but it feels right.

7

JOSEPH

*P*rez bangs the gavel on the table, and the chatter in the room dies down.

Twelve sets of eyes turn to face him, ready for our weekly meeting. We're sitting around the thick pine table, felled and carved from a tree in the local forest. The club meeting room is out the back of the Wild Taste Restaurant and overlooks the courtyard where the brewery and mechanic shop are. The colorful flags hanging outside Danni's gallery brighten the place up. She opened it a few months ago, and it's a hit with the tourists. Danni is Colter's old lady, and the entire club got behind the venture.

"First order of business. We've been asked to help Angie with renovations to her bar."

Angie lives on the other side of the mountain and

runs a restaurant and bar the same as we do. Her husband died in active service a few years ago leaving her with two kids. It was a hell of a sacrifice and we've helped her out over the years, when she lets us.

"Isn't her husband's best friend sniffing dating her now?" says Barrels.

He eyes Hops as he says it, still not comfortable with the fact that his best friend is with his sister. There are murmurs around the table and angry mutterings.

I swear this place is like a gossip house some days, grown men giving their opinion on whether a woman should stay true to her husband after he passed in the line of service. It's an uncomfortable thought, but it's been seven years. You can't expect her to stay celibate for the rest of her life.

After some discussion, we vote unanimously to help Angie. It doesn't matter what her current circumstances are. She lost her husband to this country and spent the last seven years raising their children on her own. She deserves all the help she can get.

Marcus offers to supply any timber she needs from his family sawmill, while we all pledge to help with whatever labor she needs.

There are a few other points of business, info

about a charity run we're doing in a few weeks, and then Specs goes over the accounts.

Maggie brings in a plate of pastries from the kitchen and scurries back out as quickly as she can. Our shy pastry chef is one hell of a cook but timid as heck. I notice Arlo's gaze following her out of the room.

It's when Prez asks if there's any more business that I clear my throat.

All eyes turn to me. I haven't said anything in the meeting which isn't unusual. I'm an observer and keep my opinions to myself unless asked. But this is something I need the entire club to help with.

"There's a woman staying with me."

The Prez's eyebrows shoot up his head, and some of the other guys look surprised. The fuckers. They probably think I kidnapped her or something.

"She's fleeing a bad situation, her and her baby."

My fists clench when I think about what Trish told me yesterday. How anyone can hurt a woman is beyond me, and I stayed up all night thinking about it. I promised I wouldn't go after the fucker, but I'll do all I damn well can to make sure no more harm comes to her.

I give a brief rundown on the last few days, how I found Trish, the marks on her neck, and the story she told me about her ex. I leave out the warm feeling in my chest every time I see her with the baby, the way her smile makes my insides flutter, and the way the curve of her neck makes my dick hard.

But even so, there are knowing smirks around the table. Maybe I'm not as hard to read as I think I am.

"What do you need?" asks Prez.

He's not questioning me or my actions, and I'm thankful for my MC brothers' unconditional support.

"Club protection for Trish and Rose, the baby."

Vintage shifts in his chair. "Why don't you bring them in here to stay in the clubrooms?"

The thought of sharing Trish makes me tense. I like her in my cabin where I can keep an eye on her, where I can pretend she's mine.

I shake my head. "Too many people coming in and out, and she can't keep the baby quiet. Someone might get wind of her being here."

"Is her ex looking for her?" asks Badge. He's the Sheriff of Wild and handy to have in the MC.

"Dunno," I say. "He might be happy she's gone, or he might come looking for her."

"I'll ask my team to keep an eye out."

It's hard to track strangers on the mountain

when we have tourists coming and going, but I appreciate his offer.

"She's Hailey's sister, right?" asks Hops. "When are they back?"

"No one can get ahold of them." I don't mention that I've stopped trying so hard. They might be back any day now, and my time with Trish is limited. I don't want to think about giving her up.

"But even when they're back, I want us to protect Trish."

Hops gives me a sideways smile. "You got a special interest in this woman?"

I pull at my beard and look down. I'm not ready to admit my feelings, not even to my MC brothers. But by the smirks on their faces, I can tell it's too late to hide.

"Yeah." It feels good to say it out loud. "Once I've dealt with this guy, she'll be my old lady. If she'll have me," I add.

Trish has been through a lot, and I'm not sure how she feels about me. Apart from the sweet kisses I planted on her neck yesterday, there's been no more intimacy. After what she's been through, I don't want to rush her, even though I'm aching to hold her.

There are broad smiles from around the table, and Hops slaps me on the back.

"Nice one, brother." He's grinning from ear to ear. "Love will change your life, I swear."

Barrels scowls at him. "Another pussy-whipped club member, that's all we need."

Vintage shakes his head at him. "You wait, brother. It'll happen to you one day too."

"Not likely," says Barrels. "I've got a brewery to run, and that's all I need."

Prez brings the meeting to order, and I leave the room while they vote. It's unanimous. The club will protect Trish and Rose like they're family. Relief settles over me knowing I have my brothers at my back.

The guys are staying for a drink, but there's only one place I want to be.

I'm about to leave when Prez calls me over. "I need you on the next run."

I nod and follow him to his office. It's the first time I've ever been reluctant to help with club business. But my brothers have my back, so I need to do my part.

Prez closes the door behind him, and we go over the details for the run.

8

TRISH

*I*t's been two days since Joseph found me and took me in, and in those two days, the knot of anxiety I've carried around for so long has almost eased entirely.

It's easy to be here. Joseph left this morning for a club meeting and said he'd be home after lunch.

I've spent the morning wandering the trails near his cabin with Rose strapped to my front in the sling he bought me and bear spray in one hand. Rose had her little face turned up to the sunlight streaming through the trees, as in awe of this place as I am.

She's sleeping now in the travel crib we set up in the corner of the bedroom while I clean the kitchen. It's the least I can do for the man who has taken me in, cooked me meals, and bought supplies for my baby.

He must have lived here on his own for a long time, and while the cabin appears tidy, I doubt it's ever had a deep clean.

I've pulled out all the supplies from the cupboard below the sink and I'm on my hands and knees with bright yellow cleaning gloves on.

There's a thick layer of grease, and my cloth leaves a clear path as I run through it. I sigh in satisfaction and wash the cloth out in the bucket of soapy water. Another few swipes and I've got the bottom of the cupboard back to a fresh white. I'm about to start on the cupboard door when the sound of tires crunching on gravel makes me start.

Joseph took his motorbike today, and this is definitely a car engine. My heart jumps into my throat, and I can't breathe.

How has Ian found me already?

I peer out from over the kitchen counter, and there's a huge car parked out the front of the house. It's some kind of classic old car with side wings. Not the type of car you find on the side of a mountain, but it's not Ian's beat up little Honda either.

A woman steps out of the passenger seat and she's as classic looking as the car, in a 1950s style dress with curves to match and her hair pinned up in a red scarf.

She pulls a bag out of the back and marches to the front door and knocks.

I'm frozen down on my knees, peering over the kitchen counter, not sure if I should answer it or not. I've got no idea who this strange woman is.

She shields her eyes and peers in as she knocks on the door.

"Hey," she calls. "I'm a friend of Lone Star. I've got baby clothes you can have."

At that moment Rose wakes up with a cry, and there's no point in pretending we're not here. I pop up from behind the kitchen counter and pull my gloves off.

"Just a minute."

I get Rose up before opening the door a crack.

The woman smiles when she sees Rose. "She's adorable."

Her eyes light up, and Rose smiles right back at her. "My little one's sleeping in the car; she'll be up soon."

I peer past her to where the car door hangs open, and there's the shape of a baby seat bundled up with a blanket.

"I'm Danni," the woman says. "My husband, Colter, is in the club. Thought you might need some baby things and a bit of company."

I like the woman instantly. She's got a friendly air

about her. I'm about to invite her in when there's a cry from the car.

"Ah." She pauses. "Bettie's awake. It's always the same as soon as the car stops."

She retrieves her baby from the car and jostles her on her hip, soothing the tears.

"You mind if we come in for a bit? She needs a feed."

I make a bottle for Rose while Danni feeds Bettie. They're only a few months apart, and I chat easily with Danni, sharing motherhood stories and baby tips. It's good to talk with another first time mom, and to meet one of Joseph's, or Lone Star as everyone seems to call him, friends.

While I pour Danni a coffee, I work up the courage to ask what I really want to know.

"What are the MC like?"

You hear bad stories about motorcycle clubs and what they're into, and I've only got Joseph's word to go on.

Danni nods knowingly. "They're good guys. They're not like the MCs you see on the TV."

She tells me about how her and Colter, known as Vintage, met and how the MC helped her set up her gallery and studio.

"It's like a family here. They'll do anything to help their own and protect them."

She eyes me intently, and I wonder how much Joseph has shared about my situation.

"He's a good guy, Lone Star. They call him that because he's always been a loner, but the star part is because he's loyal and true. You become his old lady, and he'll defend you to the ends of the earth."

I look down at her words, because I'm embarrassed it's that obvious what I'm thinking. That I want to stay here, that I want to hitch myself to his star and never let go.

"I've only known him for two days," I whisper, "but I don't want to leave." It feels good to confess it, to say it out loud.

Danni chuckles.

"The same thing happened to me. There's something about this mountain and the men on it. They both have a way of getting to your heart and not letting go."

Rose cries and Bettie wails in sympathy and we scoop them up, back to motherhood duties. Danni slings her baby bag over her shoulder as she holds Bettie on the other hip.

"I hope you stick around, Trish," she says before leaving. "I don't know your situation, but whatever it is, the club has your back."

As I watch her pull away in her beautiful but

impractical car, the silence of the cabin settles around me.

I could get used to life here, to the peaceful quiet of the forest. And there's something else I'm feeling: a longing in my heart, an ache in my body. Joseph's been gone for half of the day, and I miss him. There's no denying it. I'm falling for the big, silent mountain man.

9

JOSEPH

The scent of cleaning fluid and fresh flowers hits me when I open the cabin door later that afternoon.

There's a vase of wildflowers on the center of the table, and the walls of the kitchen seem brighter. The windows are thrown open, the dust gone from around the window frames.

"You cleaned up?"

Trish is on the mat with Rose, the baby giggling as she dangles the colorful caterpillar over her head. My heart warms at the giggles coming from the both of them.

"I hope you don't mind."

I don't mind at all; I could get used to this. There's a feminine touch to the cabin now. The flowers and the open windows that are streak free bring the scent of the forest into my home.

Rose makes a crying noise, and Trish picks her up.

"I'm going to get her down for her afternoon nap."

She brushes past me, and I resist the urge to reach out and pull her toward me. I want to kiss her senseless. I thought about her all day, and I love coming home to her and the baby.

While Trish puts Rose down, I fix us a snack. Every cupboard has been cleaned, the walls wiped down and the taps polished so I can see my own bristly reflection in them. Damn, it's good having Trish around.

I fix us a bowl of guacamole and grab a packet of corn chips. Trish comes out of the room a few moments later.

"She asleep already?"

It usually takes a lot longer to get Rose down. She must be settling into the place.

Trish comes into the kitchen and picks up a dish cloth. There are a few items in the drying rack, and she gets busy putting them away. I love how we move around each other easily, like she belongs in the space. She's changed into a pair of short shorts, and I can't stop glancing at her luscious thick thighs.

"Danni stopped by today."

A pang of gratitude goes through me at my MC brothers and how quickly they've mobilized to help. Trish tells me about her day and the play date the babies had. I hope it can be a regular thing for her. I hope she'll stick around.

Trish reaches up to put a pasta bowl on the top shelf and my gaze goes to her legs, getting a peek of her upper thigh as she reaches up. My breath catches in my throat. There's an angry purple bruise at the top of her thigh.

"He hit you on the legs too?"

I stride across the kitchen and crouch down to examine the bruise.

Trish spins around in shock.

"I didn't know it was still there, sorry," she whispers.

The timidity of her voice makes my blood boil.

"Honey, you've got nothing to be sorry about. The man who did this to you is a monster."

She looks down, and I hate the red blush of shame that appears on her cheeks. I want to purge her of this asshole for good. Get all the pain out of her and make her brand new, as clean and fresh as my kitchen.

I stand up slowly.

"Is there anything else I need to know about, anything else he did to you?"

Her gaze meets mine, and she holds it for a long time. Pain flickers across her face, and I hate that someone made her feel that. That she has these memories.

"I'll show you."

She hooks her thumbs under her t-shirt, and I catch her hands.

"You don't have to show me if you don't want to."

We hold each other's gazes, and in that look, I recognize trust. "I want to show you. I want you to see all of who I am."

Her words floor me. And I'm speechless as she lifts her t-shirt over her head. I feel honored that this woman trusts me enough to bare her soul to me. I don't take that lightly.

Trish's body is amazing. Full heavy breasts and a curvy stomach. My breath hitches and my throat goes dry, but I'm not here for my own needs.

There are dark finger marks on her neck, and when she turns around, a bruise on her hip.

My blood heats. How could someone do this to a woman?

"Was this the first time?"

She shakes her head. "No, but it was the worst."

The marks are under her clothing, calculated. He

probably learned this from his father, who learned it from his father before that. Generational domestic abuse that's somehow been normalized because that's all they've known.

My fists clench, thinking not just about Trish but the thousands of other women suffering in silence.

"Can I touch you?"

She nods, and I trace the marks from her neck to her hips and thighs. With every bruise my finger crosses, I make a silent vow to protect this woman with my life.

"No one will ever hurt you again, Trish. Ever."

Her eyes meet mine, and the vulnerability makes my heart break. This woman's been torn apart, and I'm going to put her back together.

I pull her into my arms. Her body is soft and tender against my large hard frame. I've never understood how a man can hurt a woman. They're smaller and softer, and we're supposed to protect them, keep them safe.

Her body molds to me, and there's a moment when the warm hug turns into something more. Her body presses against mine, and her hips move against me. My cock hardens and I step away, not wanting to add to her discomfort.

"Stay." She keeps her arms tight around me and pulls my hips toward her.

Her head tilts up, and I look down at her wide eyes. Her lips part, and we're both breathing hard. She's vulnerable. She's under my protection. I should walk away, give her space.

"Kiss me."

Her plea holds me in place. My heart thunders against my rib cage as I look down at the woman in my arms. The first person to penetrate my heart, my very soul.

She parts her lips, and there's need in her eyes.

"Are you sure?" My thumb grazes her cheek. "Because if I kiss you, there's no going back. This is for keeps, Trish. I want you as my woman, in my cabin. You and Rose."

Her eyes widen. It's a lot, I know that, but I've never been a man to do things by halves. I need her to understand that.

"I want that too." Her words stir something deep inside me, something warm and needy, a sense of belonging that I never knew I was missing.

My thumb brushes her lips, and she whimpers. I wonder how long it's been since she was touched the way a woman should be touched.

My lips press to hers, and warmth spreads through my veins. It's a slow kiss, tender and gentle. There's a lot of healing that needs doing, and I won't give in to my animal instincts until she's ready. My hands slide down her back, tangling in her hair as I touch every part of her, needing to feel her skin against mine.

She tastes like coffee and baby milk, and it's my new favorite flavor.

Her hands hook under my t-shirt, and she pulls it over my head. Her hips grind against mine and my dick responds, pushing against my jeans until I think the seams will burst.

But this isn't about me. Trish needs to be shown love. She needs to be worshipped the way she deserves.

Her fingers pull at my belt buckle, but I stop them with my hands. She looks up at me, confused.

"I'm gonna give you what you deserve, Trish. I'm gonna show you how a man's supposed to treat a woman."

10

TRISH

*J*oseph sinks to his knees, his palms scraping over my thighs as he does. There is so much running through my head right now: Should I be doing this? What if Rose wakes up? When's the last time I shaved *down there*?

But all thoughts flee my brain when his warm breath caresses the skin of my thigh. I gasp at the sensation of his beard scratching against my delicate skin as his soft lips work their way up my thigh. He gets to the top of my shorts and yanks them down, exposing my threadbare cotton panties.

His hands caress the gusset, and his breath catches.

"You're already wet."

I've been wet for this man since he took me in.

Kissing Joseph feels like a relief, confirmation that my feelings over the last few days are real, that he feels them too.

But as his fingers run between my legs and his breath hits my thighs, the warmth I felt at the kiss turns to pure pleasure. The knot in my stomach disappears completely, and a new sensation begins to build. A beautiful carefree sensation that I haven't felt in a long time. As his fingers slide under my panties, I feel like I'm floating, like I don't have to worry about anything. For this moment, it's all about me and my pleasure.

I barely notice Joseph peeling my panties off and slinging my leg over his shoulder. We're still in the kitchen, and I grab hold of the counter with one hand as his tongue licks my swollen folds. My thighs clench together, not used to having a man down there.

Joseph sits back on his haunches, his gaze on my pussy.

"You're beautiful, Trish."

No one's ever worshipped me down there like he is.

Joseph nudges my thighs apart and I open for him, feeling vulnerable but in safe hands. He dips his head with reverence and slowly kisses the most intimate parts of me. His tongue slides into my opening, and he groans at the same time I moan.

The fact that he's getting off on this as much as I am helps me relax. I lean back, letting him take care of me. Meaty hands grab my butt, and he pulls me onto his face. His beard tickles me between the legs as his tongue flicks over every part of me.

It's erotic and dirty, and I want so much more of him. Feeling bold, I grind my pussy into his face. Joseph responds by sliding a finger inside me. My pussy sucks in his digit as the pressure builds inside my walls.

I lean back, gripping the counter as my moans echo around the kitchen. He's devouring me like I'm his favorite dessert, and it feels so good I can't hold on much longer.

Then I'm over the edge. Stars burst in my vision, and I stifle a cry. Waves of pleasure wash over me, and my spirit soars. For the first time in months I'm truly free, my body taking something for itself.

As the orgasm subsides, Joseph presses his face to me once more. I grab his hair and move his head where I need it, riding his face with a new confidence. It doesn't take long for another orgasm to claim me. My pussy pulses on his tongue, and he licks my juices up hungrily.

Only when my body is exhausted does he let up.

He lowers my leg and stands up, wiping my juices off his beard.

I reach for the bulge in his jeans, wanting to return the favor, but he shakes his head.

"Tonight is all about you, Trish. Showing you how you deserve to be treated."

It's hard to believe his words. The only other man I've known is Ian, and he never did what Joseph just did. It's hard to believe there are men this good in the world, let alone that I've fallen for one.

My heart fills with gratitude and I push off the counter, but my legs buckle under me.

Joseph catches me in his arms.

"You must be exhausted."

He's not wrong. The exhaustion from the last several months has finally caught up with me. Living on the edge, never sleeping properly in case something happened to Rose. For the first time in months, I feel truly relaxed, and it makes my body heavy.

"Let's get you to bed."

Joseph leads me to the bedroom and I lean into him, feeling safe and satisfied.

"Stay with me tonight," I say, not wanting him to sleep on the couch.

"Trish, I'll spend every night with you for the rest of my life if you ask me to."

After checking Rose, I crawl into bed and Joseph wraps his arms around me. My body relaxes completely. I have him, and my daughter is safe. There is nothing to be anxious about. I fall into a deep, dreamless sleep.

11

JOSEPH

A mewling noise drags me from my slumber. The bed shifts next to me, and I smile as memories of last night fill my head. The taste of Trish's sweet pussy, the way she came, dancing on my tongue, and the release I gave her that she so desperately needed. And how we fell asleep, her warm body molded against mine like it was always meant to be there.

Rose's cries drag me from the memory, and I flick on the bedside light.

"Sorry," Trish whispers, "I'll take her out to the living room and change her."

She cradles Rose to her chest, but the baby doesn't stop crying.

"Don't apologize." I swing my legs over the side

of the bed and catch her arm before she can scurry out.

"Change her here."

She kisses the top of Rose's head and rubs her back, trying to calm her. I smile. I'll never get sick of the sight of the two of them in my cabin, even at five o'clock in the morning.

"Don't ever apologize," I say. "This is where you and Rose belong now, Trish. Don't apologize for the needs of your daughter."

She gives me a grateful look as she grabs the changing mat, and a flare of anger goes off inside me. That asshole ex of hers probably hated the baby crying. From what Trish has told me, he blamed her for Rose's crying instead of helping out with the baby like a parent should.

"I've got traps to check anyways."

Getting out in the woods will help with the rage I feel toward that scumbag. I've been neglecting my traps and haven't been hunting for the last few days. I need to get out to see if there are any animals I need to process.

Rose's cries have turned to giggles as she makes a grab for Trish's hair. Trish distracts her as she changes the diaper, shaking her head so her hair tickles Rose's face.

"She's wide awake now." Trish sighs. "I guess that's all the sleep I'm getting tonight."

But she's got a smile on her face, and who can blame her? Her daughter's giggles are infectious.

"You two climb back into bed. I'll fix you a bottle and a coffee."

"You don't need to do that, Joseph."

Trish efficiently puts the changing mat away all with one hand cradling her daughter. She doesn't get it yet. She doesn't get that I'll do anything for her and the baby.

I slide my arm around her waist and pull them both toward me.

Rose looks up at me in surprise. Her little hand reaches out and grabs my beard. When she tugs on it, her eyes open wide in shock at the way it feels. Then she giggles and yanks on it again.

"You got some strength in you." I chuckle at the little girl. "You'll make a good hunter one day."

I've learned a few things about babies over the last few days, and it doesn't take me long to mix the formula and get the bottle heating. While the milk's warming, I put the coffee on.

It won't be light for another hour or so, but I love getting up in the predawn and getting out into the forest. Having a baby around the house suits me better than I ever thought it would. I'm used to early mornings.

When I go back to the bedroom, Trish is sitting up in bed singing nursery rhymes to Rose. I put the coffee down on the bedside table and hand her the bottle. Rose reaches for it greedily.

Before heading out, I stop at the bedroom door and spend a long moment watching them, Rose sucking hungrily while Trish sings softly to her daughter. My heart warms, and my chest expands. They're everything I never knew I needed in my life. And I hope to hell I can make them mine.

Frost crunches under my boots as I head into the forest. The well-worn paths crisscross in the undergrowth and today I take the east track, planning to circle around to check each of my traps.

When I came to Wild Heart Mountain, I bought this piece of land covered in forest. I know it intimately and I've come to love it, the wildlife, the trees, the weather patterns.

I'm already thinking about how I'll share it with Trish and Rose. The family walks I'll take them on. I'll teach Trish how to hunt and how to trap, how to live off the land.

My thoughts are flooded with the future as I come to the first trap.

There's a bunny in it, a big one that'll give us meat for the winter. I usually sell the pelts in town, but I'll make something for Rose out of this one, a blanket and some mittens to keep her warm for the winter that's coming.

Rabbit hide will make a good underlay for the crib, which I'll have to build. There are a couple of pines near the cabin where the wood will be perfect.

The cabin will need extending, but that can wait till the spring. I don't mind having Rose sleep with us for a few months.

We'll need a room for Rose and maybe more rooms for mine and Trish's kids.

The thought has me smiling. A few days ago, I would have run at the sight of a baby. But since meeting Trish, there's nothing I want more than to see my home filled with children. Our children. And I already count Rose among my own. I feel as responsible for her as I do for her mother.

With more mouths to feed and a bigger family, I'll have to hunt more. I'll extend the veggie garden, and we'll get a couple of chickens for fresh eggs. It'll be an adjustment, but my heart warms at the thought of Trish, belly round with a baby inside her, tending to the veggie patch.

. . .

It's a few hours later, and I'm on my way back with four bunnies strung over one shoulder and my hunting rifle over the other. There was no sign of deer today, but there's always tomorrow.

I'm whistling as I walk, thinking about insulating the cabin. With winter coming and a baby to take care of, I'll need to make some improvements.

I'm smiling to myself thinking about this new future as I come out of the thicket of trees near my cabin. I stop in my tracks.

There's a flicker of white through the trees, a car that I don't recognize. I drop to my knees and shrug the rabbits onto the ground.

My heart's racing, but my military training kicks in. Silently, I ease the rifle off my shoulder and move forward across the forest.

The car is a beat up Honda and not one that I recognize. I'll bet you anything that's her asshole ex.

I whip my phone out and make a quick call to Prez, thankful that I installed a satellite dish on the cabin.

I explain the situation to the Prez and tell him I'm going in. The MC will be here as soon as they can, but I don't know what's happening inside the cabin and I need to get to Trish and Rose.

Dumping everything but the hunting rifle, I creep closer to the cabin.

From what Trish has told me about Ian, he's the kind of guy who would bully a woman but shit his pants if he came up against anyone his own size. Well, he's going to get the scare of his life. I want him to see who Trish has in her corner now, that there's an entire MC protecting her.

But I have to be cautious. He's a man with a wounded ego. His girlfriend and baby left him. That must hurt, and there's no telling what he might do.

The front door is open a crack, and I push it all the way open with the barrel of my gun. Voices are coming from the bedroom mixed with the sound of Rose's cries. My heart hammers against my chest and I want to rush in there, but I've got surprise on my side. And as I learned in the military, surprise can go a long way in deciding an outcome.

I'm a big guy, but I can be stealthy when I need to. I creep through the cabin until I'm at the door of the bedroom. Keeping low to the ground, I edge the door open until I get a full picture of the situation.

A tall man with greasy hair holds Rose in front of him as the baby screams and writhes in his arms. Her face is puckered, and her arms reach out for her momma.

"Just hand me Rose, please." Trish's eyes are wide and terrified, and I hate the desperation in her voice.

Her eyes are only on Rose, and she doesn't see me at first.

"Make her fucking stop, Trish. Tell her to stop fucking crying."

Ian jiggles the baby harder, making Rose scream.

"Give her to me and I'll make her stop, I promise." Trish reaches for Rose, but Ian holds her out of Trish's grasp.

My instinct is to shoot the fucker for what he's done, but he's holding Rose and she can't get hurt. I lower my gun and rise to my feet; I'll do this the old fashioned way.

This guy must be deaf as well as stupid, because he doesn't hear me sneak up behind him. Trish's eyes glance at me and I hold my finger out for her to be quiet, to not let him know I'm here.

I give her a nod, and we move at the same time. I barrel into Ian as Trish lunges forward and snatches Rose out of his hands.

Ian spins around just in time for my fist to connect with his face. He screams, which makes Rose scream louder.

"Get her out of here."

Trish cradles Rose to her chest and scoots past us out of the bedroom. As I lay into Ian, my vision goes red as all the rage simmering inside me comes out in my fists. I pummel the man who hurt the woman I love, and when he slumps to the floor, I kick him.

"You motherfucker."

Kick

"You think it's fun to hurt a woman."

Kick

"You're scum."

Kick

All the rage I've pent up since I saw Trish's bruise comes out of me. I've seen humans hurt each other. I've seen humans shoot each other and beat each other to death. In the military I learned how to fight and I learned how to kill. And that's where I go now. My years of training and the unofficial training I had from what I witnessed goes into each kick.

"Stop!"

Trish's voice cuts through my rage.

My foot pauses mid kick. Ian's in the fetal position on the floor, his arms covering his head as blood spurts from his nose. My boot is covered in his sticky blood, and there's an acrid smell from where he's pissed his pants.

I hate this man for what he did to Trish and Rose, but if I let my anger go and kill him, then I'm no better than him. I'm no better than the dehumanized soldiers from both sides who I witnessed doing bad things to each other.

But there is good in this world. I've witnessed it in the last few days, seeing Trish's devotion to her baby and the MC coming together to help. Since I've lived on Wild Heart Mountain, I've only seen the good side of humanity. And maybe that's what humanity mostly is. Maybe what I witnessed was the exception.

If I take Ian's life, I'm no better than the dark side of humanity that I fear, but in the last few days I've seen the light. I've got something to live for now, an example to set for my family, for my daughter.

I stagger backward, breathing hard. Trish puts a hand on my shoulder and it's reassuring, her light in my darkness.

From out front comes the roar of bikes.

"You're not worth going to prison for." I grab Ian by his T-shirt and haul him to his feet.

He pleads with me not to hurt him as I shove him towards the door.

"There's nothing for you here, you understand? You lost your right to be with this woman and this baby."

He's blubbering, snot bubbling out of his nose mixed with blood. I almost feel sorry for him until he speaks.

"She took my money."

I'm so angry I almost hit him again. He loses a

woman like Trish and his own baby, and all he can think about is the money that Trish took off him.

I pull a few bills out of my pocket and shove them at him. I don't want to give him any excuse to come back.

"Here's your money, asshole."

By this time we've reached the front door where Hops, Barrels, and Prez are getting off their bikes. The roar of engines coming up the path bring three more of my brothers.

Badge is absent, which is for the best. Plausible deniability if this loser is stupid enough to make a complaint.

If Ian was scared before, he's terrified now.

We're an impressive sight, my boys in leather patches with their big road bikes.

Trish comes onto the porch cradling Rose and the MC stand in front of her, forming a barrier.

Ian swivels his bleeding head between us with wide eyes, no doubt wondering what the fuck he's walked into. His gaze finds Trish and he looks vulnerable, like the schoolboy she must have fallen for.

"Come back, Trish," he says. "I miss you."

The fucker seems genuine, which pisses me off. How typical that he doesn't realize what he's got until he it's gone. I turn to Trish. There's no way in hell I'll let her go off with this scumbag, but he needs to hear it from her.

She steps forward, clutching Rose to her chest.

"It's over, Ian. Whatever we had. It's been over for a long time. I'm taking our daughter, and I never want to see you again."

Ian's face is a picture of agony. But I have no sympathy for this asshole. I shove him down the steps, and he staggers to his car.

I follow him, flanked by Barrels and Wood, until he gets into his shitty Honda. I'm proud to see Trish standing tall on the porch. Rose has stopped crying, and with my MC club flanking her, they look formidable.

Ian gets in his car and kicks up the gravel in a hurry to get out of here. Without being asked, Barrels and Wood get on their bikes and follow, giving him a personal escort off the mountain.

It's not till he's gone that my fists unclench.

I stride to my woman and put my hands on her shoulders, scanning her and Rose for any signs of harm.

"Are you okay?"

She's trembling but she juts her chin out, and I love how strong she is, not wanting to give him the power and setting a good example for her daughter.

"We're good. Thank you."

"I mean it, Trish. I want you to stay here with me. I don't want to be another man telling you what to do. But if you want it, there's a place for you here. You and Rose. I love you, Trish. And I'll protect you for the rest of my life."

Her bottom lip wobbles, and now the tears come. She buries her face in my chest, and I put my arm around her and Rose.

Prez catches my eye as he slips his phone into his pocket.

"Badge has got a team following the car to make sure it gets out of town. His plate will be on a watch list if he ever tries to get close again."

"He won't be that stupid."

I think about the kicking I gave him; how easy it would have been to keep going. But I didn't. I stopped. When it came to it, I was one of the good guys.

12
TRISH

 *M*y hands shake as I clutch Rose to my chest, her little heartbeat thundering against mine.

"It's okay." I rub her back, but I'm not sure if I'm soothing her or myself.

The relief at seeing Ian go makes my legs weak, and I cling to Joseph.

"Are you okay?" he asks.

It takes me a moment to answer. I think about Ian turning up, surprising us, and the fear that sliced through me when he took Rose. Then the relief when Joseph turned up.

I wasn't sorry to see Ian getting a beating, but I'm glad that it's over. He's a coward, and with the MC here he won't be back. Finally, I've got him out of my life.

"Do you need anything?"

I look up to the kindly face of one of the MC guys. I'm so relieved they turned up.

"We're fine. But do you want some coffee? Please, stay for breakfast."

I glance at Joseph, just realizing that I've offered his food up for everyone. I've gotten so comfortable here that it feels like my own home.

Joseph just smiles at me. "Yup," he says. "Least we can do is get you some breakfast."

I carry Rose inside and put her in the sling. She's wide awake, but I want to keep her close to me.

There's a carton of eggs in the cupboard and bacon in the fridge, and I get to work making breakfast for the men who showed up to help a stranger.

Joseph introduces me to his MC friends. They've all got two names. Travis has the road name Hops and works with Barrels, whose real name is Quentin.

Arlo's road name is Prince, as in Prince Charming. I can see why. He's younger than the others with a cheeky smile that he gives freely. He takes Rose off me, and she giggles as the big man throws her up in the air, charming my little girl. Colter introduces himself as the husband of Danni. He invites us over anytime we like for a play date.

There isn't enough room inside, so we take our breakfasts onto the porch and eat on the stairs.

Joseph takes Rose on his knee, and he puts a bit of runny egg on his finger. Her face screws up when she licks it, making the men laugh.

Everyone talks easily, and as I listen to the chatter of the men, my heart lifts. I feel safe here. It's a real family, and they've welcomed me with open arms.

A little while later, we wave off the last of the MC.

Rose is exhausted, and I give her a bottle and put her down for a nap.

When I come out of the bedroom, Joseph's on the porch, and I join him. We sit in companionable silence on the two rocking chairs, looking out at the forest and listening to the bird song.

He reaches across the chair and takes my hand.

"I meant everything I said, Trish. I want you here with the baby. I want to have our own babies with you. But it's got to be your decision."

It's not a hard decision. It's peaceful here, it's safe, and I've fallen for the quiet recluse with the kind heart. There's just one thing that's niggling at me.

"If you hadn't have found me on Hailey's doorstep, I don't know what I would have done."

He squeezes my hand. "There's no point thinking about that. That's not how it happened."

But he misunderstands what I'm getting at.

"I was lucky, Joseph. I had somewhere I could go. I had Hailey. But there are a lot of women with nowhere to go. Nowhere to run to."

An idea has been percolating in my mind for the last few days, but I don't know how to make it a reality.

"What if there was somewhere in the mountains, a refuge for woman and their children. Somewhere they knew they could escape to, no questions asked."

I'd hate for a woman to be in my situation and not be able to leave because she didn't know where to go.

Joseph looks at me thoughtfully. "Aren't there places like that already?"

"Yes. But not here."

I look out to the depths of the forest, the light that breaks through the clearing. "There's something healing about the mountains. They make you think. They connect you with nature and remind you there's a better life."

Joseph sits back in his chair and pulls on his beard. "The club's got some spare land near the compound. I could talk to the guys."

My heart leaps. I can't believe he's taking me seriously.

"It's all well and good, having a refuge in the mountains, but if it was run by a gang of burly ex-military bikers, you wouldn't get many assholes turning up looking for trouble."

My mouth drops open. I never thought about getting the MC involved, but he's right. What better protection than the Wild Riders MC?

My heart lifts with something I haven't felt in a long time, and it takes me a while to recognize it as hope. Hope for myself and hope for Rose, but also hope for other women in a bad situation that there might be something I could do to help.

"I love you."

The words slip out, and I clap my hand over my mouth. Joseph's eyes sparkle, and a rare smile spreads across his face.

"I love you too, honey."

He kisses me then, long and deep. I let out a sigh as our lips meet, and heat spreads through me.

Joseph pulls me out of my chair and onto his lap.

The baby's asleep, and we're outside. There's no one else here, just the forest, the birds and the breeze, the fresh air against my cheeks.

I wiggle my butt against him, feeling him harden

under me. The heat between us is scorching as he kisses me hard.

Just then, my phone rings. I try to ignore it until I remember Hailey.

Jumping off Joseph, I grab my phone from inside.

"I just got your message. My god Trish, I'm so sorry."

She's frantic, and it takes me a while to calm her down and make her believe everything's all right.

I fill her in quickly about what happened, and she's horrified that she missed me until I tell her I've been staying with Joseph. It's awkward talking about him when he's right there, but I don't need to say much. My sister knows. She squeals with delight, and we make a promise to visit this afternoon.

I love my sister, but it's a relief to hang up the phone. Joseph's waiting for me with hungry eyes.

"Where were we?"

He sidles off the chair and sits on the porch steps and pulls me onto his lap, and this time I straddle him.

"I was about to make you my woman."

13
JOSEPH

*T*rish straddles me on the porch, her thighs scraping against my own. She gyrates slowly, pressing her hips into me and turning my cock to steel.

My hands run up her back and tangle in her hair, pulling her head back so I can kiss her neck. She moans at my touch as I nibble at the skin of her throat.

I've waited so long for this woman, and now she's mine. She's mine. For real and forever.

We fumble at each other's clothes, and I pull her T-shirt off her head. She pulls my shirt off, and the cool air dances across my chest.

I shuffle around so that I'm sitting with my feet on the first step and she's straddling me with her feet on the next step down, keeping her hips in a good position and giving me access to her pussy.

I unhook her bra, and her luscious tits pop free. My mouth moves over them, and I suck on her nipples one by one. The little whimpers that come out of her mouth drive me crazy.

"You can be loud out here, Trish. There's no one here but the trees and wildlife."

"You think the bunnies are watching?" She giggles, and it's the first carefree sound I've heard come out of her. I want to hear it again.

"Nah, not the bunnies. It's the deer that like to watch."

She laughs again and I capture her mouth, wanting to kiss that giggle and trap it forever inside me.

Her giggles turn to moans as I move my mouth down her throat and to her breasts.

My teeth scrape her nipple as I roll the other one around in my fingertips. Her hips buck at every movement, and her moans peak into little cries.

God, she's got sensitive nipples, and I fucking love that. I want to find every sensitive spot on her body and work it until she begs for mercy.

Her hands snake down my chest, fingertips running over every muscle and tangling in my chest hair. She tugs on it slightly and pricks of pain jolt through my body, making me gasp.

Her eyes go wide with delight at the discovery that she can get little noises out of me.

I love this exploration and I could explore her body all day, but right now there's something I need more.

I tug at her leggings, and she lifts her butt so I can slide her leggings and panties off. Then she's tugging at my jeans.

We stand up so we can dispose of our clothing, and when I sit back, it's on the porch.

She's standing before me naked, and my breath hitches. I can't breathe. She's a vision, this beautiful woman who came into my life, who's mine to keep, mine to protect. The bruising on her body has faded, and I swear to God, I will never let anyone harm her again.

"Come here, beautiful."

She moves forward slowly, shyly. I put my hands on her buttocks and breathe in the scent of arousal.

"Part your legs for me, honey."

She's standing above me, and she does as I ask. I look up into her eyes.

"I'm going to worship at your temple every day, Trish. You're beautiful, and you deserve to be worshipped."

I pull her butt towards me and slide her pussy onto my tongue, tipping my head back to get better access. I lean back and rest one hand on the porch as Trish shuffles forward. She grabs hold of the back of the rocking chair and spreads her legs wide for me. She's so fucking sexy, standing over me, her hips moving while she rides my tongue.

I've seen her confidence grow in the last few days. She's not the frightened mother I found. This woman I've got dancing on the end of my tongue is all confidence. I glance up as I move my tongue and appreciate the glorious sight of her tits bouncing above me.

Our eyes meet, and one hand slides down over her breasts. Her thumb brushes her nipple, and her eyes roll backwards as she moans.

I fucking love it that she's playing with herself. While Trish works her tits, I bring my hand up and slide it between her folds, slipping a finger inside her pussy.

She's so fucking tight and wet. Her juices flow over my tongue and dribble into my beard.

I can't take it slow; I need to warm her up so that she's ready for my cock, which is hard as the wood I'm sitting on.

I lick and I suck, and I find her clit and flick it

with my tongue as my finger pumps in and out of her.

"Joseph..." she moans, and I love the way she says my name.

I love the way that the breeze whips her hair, strands falling over her tits. There's bird song around us, and being outside with the forest surrounding us adds to my urgency.

"Joseph..."

Her voice is high pitched, and I can tell she's close.

I slide another finger inside and finger fuck her good while my tongue flicks her hard nub.

She's writhing on my face, hips jerking back and forth as she slides her pussy up and down my tongue.

"Joseph..."

She pants my name over and over, and it's the sweetest sound I've ever fucking heard.

Then her pussy convulses, and she's screaming my name into the forest. Her juice explodes on my tongue and I lick it all up, not wasting a drop.

I don't even wait for her to stop trembling before I pull her down to me. She straddles my lap, and her eyes bulge at the sight of my ramrod straight cock aiming straight for her sweet spot.

"You ready for me, Trish?"

She nods, and that's all I need. Grabbing her hips, I pull her down hard, impaling her pussy on my aching cock.

As I sink into her, I let out a groan. Heat washes over me, and she feels so fucking good, so tight and wet that every nerve ending in my cock is standing on end.

Our eyes meet as I slide her slowly off my cock, then thrust her back down.

"Joseph..." She cries out, her eyes roll back in her head, and her fingernails dig into my shoulder. I jerk her up and down my shaft as her tits bounce in my face, loving the feeling of her hungry pussy squeezing my cock.

Her moans get high pitched again, and I rock her back and forth so her clit brushes against my body.

"I'm gonna come again."

Which is the sweetest thing I ever heard.

"Come for me, Trish, before I shoot my load inside you."

She whimpers. Then her pussy tightens, and she's screaming my name as the orgasm races through her.

My cock lengthens, and I thrust deep into her. My cum shoots into her pussy in thick, hot ropes. As she screams my name, I let out a roar, bellowing into the woods like a rutting buck. Letting all the forest know that I claim this woman. Holding Trish close, I pump every last drop into her.

I've seen my woman with a baby, and now I want to see her pregnant. I want to see a baby in her belly and Rose in her arms.

We stay like that for a long time, panting and holding each other, naked on the cabin porch.

It's the cries of Rose that bring us apart.

But I don't begrudge her. I feel happy. I feel satisfied. I've got my woman; I've got a little family of my own. It's more than this loner ever thought he'd have.

EPILOGUE

TRISH

One year later...

Sweat sticks to my palms and I wipe them on my maternity leggings, hoping they don't leave a mark for the cameras.

Joseph puts a reassuring arm around my shoulder.

"You ready?"

His sparkling eyes are full of a confidence in me that I wish I felt. I let out a deep breath and pull my spine up as tall as my protruding belly will allow.

"Let's do this."

I step into the sunlight and falter when I see the line of cameras and waiting press. My gaze lifts behind them to the line of Wild Riders, their wives and Hailey. There are other people from the mountain who I recognize. The entire community has turned out for the opening of the center, and the support gives me courage and makes me stand taller.

I step confidently to the podium and waiting cameras. Joseph never leaves my side, glaring at anyone who gets too close.

He grumbled at me opening the center when I was eight months pregnant, but I reasoned it's better to get it up and running before the baby arrives. The center needs publicity, and I need to get the word out there to whoever needs to hear it.

The Wild Riders MC agreed to help fund the center. They leased me land near their compound and helped build the cabins that make up the retreat.

It's nestled in the woods, surrounded by a large fence and at least two Wild Riders on security at all times. The place really feels like a refuge.

The location is nondisclosed, which is why we're doing the press conference at the Wild Riders HQ. In the pamphlets and social ads, I give the same message. Go to the Hope train station and call the number I give out. We have volunteers on the mountain 24/7 ready to give a lift when a call comes in. Women and their children can stay as long as they need.

After the press conference, Hailey takes over, leading the press through to the bar, where there's a screening of a video we shot showing the facilities but being careful to hide any identifiable landmarks.

Maggie's done the catering, and Kendra helped plan the opening. I've got a team of mountain women who have helped me get this project off the ground, and I'm thankful for every one of them.

I'll join them inside soon for any further questions, but the hardest part of my day is over.

Danni has been watching Rose, who's an active one year old now. She hands her over to Joseph, and my daughter laughs as her father swings her into the air. He's the only father Rose will ever know, and that's fine by me. Ian didn't even try to get access to his daughter, not that I'd have let him. I haven't heard from him since he left the mountain. Badge made sure his team memorized Ian's license plate, and if he's stupid enough to set foot on the mountain again, he'll be notified.

Badge also took my statement and pictures of the bruises to keep on file in case I ever want to file a report.

I barely give Ian a second thought these days. I'm too busy. With our expanding family and the center to set up, it's been a hectic few months.

The knot in my stomach tightens, which is weird, because the press conference that I've been nervous about is out of the way.

My stomach clenches, and I gasp.

"What is it?" Joseph's at my side instantly, cradling Rose in his arms.

I look down to the puddle of water on the ground. His gaze follows mine.

"Oh shit."

I've never seen my husband look so terrified, and I bark out a laugh.

"Prez!" he shouts, and every member of the MC turns at his tone.

"I need a van and a driver."

He practically throws Rose at Danni as he lifts me into his arms. I'm already a curvy girl and when you add the baby in my belly, it's enough to make even Joseph stumble.

"I can walk."

I laugh as I bat his shoulder, but he won't put me down. It's useless to try to change his mind, so I relax in his arms as he carries me to the van that Prez has ordered into the courtyard.

"It's early. Why is it early?"

Joseph is seriously freaking out, and I try to explain that due dates are pretty random but he's too panicked. My laugh turns to a grimace as another contraction squeezes my insides.

Joseph practically throws me into the back of the van, and I just have time to buckle up before we take off. Luckily Arlo is driving and not my panicked husband.

Joseph's next to me in the backseat, and I grip his hand as another contraction washes over me.

"Breathe, honey, breathe." I hold his hand and do some breathing exercises, which he seems to need more than me.

The contractions are closer together than they should be, and I don't want to panic Joseph anymore but I have to ask.

"How long until we reach the hospital?"

"About thirty minutes," Arlo calls from the front seat.

The closest is the medical center in Hope, but I don't think we're going to make it in time. I cling on to Joseph as the contractions get closer together, and try to focus on the scenery as it speeds by.

As we bump down the mountain road and into Hope, I'm panting hard and ready to push.

I catch sight of Joseph's panicked face. I can't help giggling, even though I'm in pain and about to give birth in the back of a van.

"What you laughing at?" He looks at me like I'm crazy, and in this moment, I feel like I am.

"I hope you're ready to meet your daughter, because she's coming."

The last thing I see is Joseph's wide eyes. Then

I'm pushing and panting, and a few moments later a screaming red bundle drops right into his lap.

We stare at the puckered red face in silence. Then the mouth opens, and an almighty scream comes from its lips.

Joseph holds up his new daughter. His panicked expression has turned to wonder.

My mountain man saved me when I was lost, and now I'm giving him the greatest gift I can give. A family.

* * *

BONUS SCENE

Can't bear to say good bye to Joseph and Trish just yet? Want to see what happens when the former recluse Lone Star has a cabin full of girls?

Get the free bonus scene for a sneak peek into Joseph and Trish's family life.

Read the bonus scene when you sign up to the Sadie King mailing list.

To sign up visit: authorsadieking.com/bonus-scenes

Already a subscriber? Check your last email for the link to access all the bonus content.

A fake relationship for a weekend between a biker who wants more and a shy girl who can't give him the one thing he craves...

Mom's coming to visit, and she expects to meet my new boyfriend. Spoiler alert: I don't have a boyfriend. I pretended I had one to get Mom off my back. I didn't expect her to show up on the mountain to meet him.

In steps Arlo, the bearded, tattooed biker I've been crushing on since I started working at the Wild Riders MC HQ. We'll pretend to be together to keep Mom happy. But as the weekend goes on, I'm falling for the easy-going ex-military biker.

But there's a reason why I don't date, and not even Arlo can change my mind.

Wild Curves is a fake relationship romance featuring an ex-military mountain man biker and the shy girl whose curves he can't get enough of.

WILD CURVES

CHAPTER ONE

Maggie

My hand shakes as I place the plate of chocolate-coated strawberries on the bar counter.

Arlo gives me an encouraging look that makes my insides flutter. I look away quickly, hoping he thinks my nerves are because of the dessert I'm presenting and not the fact that his luminous smile is turned on me.

"Let's give them a taste."

My attention snaps to Travis as he snags one of the strawberries and stuffs it in his mouth. He's the boss of the Wild Taste Bar and Restaurant and the person I have to impress if I want to get the pastry chef position once Patrick retires at the end of the year.

I hold my breath as he chews. His brows knit together and then raise in surprise.

"There's chili in these?"

I nod. "A little, to offset the sweetness."

"Mmmm…" Travis nods appreciatively. "These are good." He reaches for another one, and Kendra slaps his hand out of the way.

"Leave some for the rest of us."

She's the only one who can get away with playfully slapping the boss. He picks one up anyway and brings it to her lips.

Kendra opens her mouth to receive the strawberry and Travis pulls it away, just out of her reach. They both giggle and I look away, my ears turning pink at the intimacy of the moment.

Arlo catches my gaze and rolls his eyes heavenwards, making me smile. He works the bar and makes no secret of how sick he is of seeing Kendra and Travis all over each other since they got together.

I think it's sweet, the boss and the head waitress.

"What did you say these are called?" Arlo asks.

The blush spreads up my neck, and heat blooms in my cheeks.

"They're um… Strawberry Sin."

Arlo's eyes go wide, and a smile curls up his lips. "They taste like sin too."

As he says it he bites into the strawberry, breaking the chocolate seal with his teeth. My eyes dart to his lips. Lips so full they look indecent on a man. Lips so full they haunt my dreams as I imagine what they taste like, strawberry and chocolate with a hint of chili and cardamom. Sweetness and heat and something manly and exotic, which was my inspiration for the dessert. My knees go weak and my blush deepens.

"I need to get back to the kitchen and clean up."

I scurry away before the sight of Arlo enjoying the dessert that he was the inspiration for causes me to melt right onto the restaurant floor.

When I'm safely back in the kitchen, I lean so my forearms rest on the silver bench and let the coolness of the metal calm my heated skin.

All bartenders are terrible flirts, I tell myself. He likes my desserts and that's all.

Through the round window of the swinging kitchen door that leads to the restaurant, I watch as my three colleagues enjoy the rest of my strawberry sins.

I've been working at the Wild Taste for three months now, and any normal person would be out there chatting and laughing with their colleagues. The last customer left a half hour ago, and while they've been out there enjoying their drinks, I asked if I could present Travis with a dessert I've been working on.

I should be out there socializing, but I prefer the cool steadiness of the kitchen. Especially after hours when everyone else has gone home.

My phone rings, and I stifle a groan when I see it's Mom calling.

I contemplate slipping it back in my pocket, but I've already missed two calls from her today. She'll get frantic if I don't pick up.

"Hi Mom."

"Maggie!" She screeches so loud that I pull the phone away from my ear. "I couldn't get hold of you."

"I'm working, Mom. Didn't you get my text?"

"You know I find it hard to read those things. Call me old-fashioned, but I prefer to talk."

Old-fashioned is definitely the word I'd use to describe my mother. And if this call is anything like the daily calls I get, I brace myself for what I'm in for.

"You work too hard, sweetheart. Make sure you leave time for yourself to have some fun."

I lick a bit of chocolate off my hand and try not to roll my eyes.

"Working is fun for me. I've invented a new dessert."

I try to sound upbeat, but as usual Mom pays zero interest to my professional life.

"You'll never meet anyone if you're working all the time, MeMe."

She uses my pet name from childhood and the stern but kindly tone that my mother has perfected.

It's incomprehensible to my mother that I would put my career ahead of meeting a suitable husband. This is usually where I tell her I don't want to meet anyone, and she gasps like she's having a heart attack. But I can't do it today.

We've had this same conversation for the last two years, since I went to culinary school and told her I wanted to be a pastry chef.

"And your uterus isn't getting any younger, sweetheart. Fertility starts to decline after thirty, you know."

The last is said in a whisper as if someone might hear her down the phone lines.

"Mom, that's not really true…"

"It is," she protests. "I read it in a magazine. These women putting their careers first…"

She launches into a tirade spoken in hushed but disapproving tones about 'these women' when what she really means is me.

"Mom…" I try to cut in to remind her that I'm

only twenty-three, but as always, I'm no match for my mother once she gets on a roll.

It's been a week of early double shifts, and the tiredness behind my eyes shifts to a full blown headache as I listen to my mom drone on. I press my fingers to my forehead and close my eyes, knowing from experience that it's best to let her run on until she's finished.

I love my mother, but it's the same lecture every week. Her first reaction when I told her I wanted to be a chef was how difficult the odd hours would be for raising a family.

I hadn't thought about that aspect of working life before. I just wanted to choose a career doing something I loved. Mom brings it up so often that I guess it's true.

As Mom drones on about the declining health of my ovaries, I watch Arlo through the window. He's chatting easily with Travis and Kendra, and a pang of longing jolts my insides. I shake it off. Mom's made it abundantly clear to me that if I want to be a pastry chef I'll never have a family. That's why I don't date. Even if the ridiculously handsome and charming bartender had an interest in small, tubby shy girls, there wouldn't be any point in dating him.

My head aches, and I want to get off this call with Mom and find out what they really thought of my dessert and if Travis will put it on the menu. If only there was a way to get Mom off my back once and for all.

"I want a promise from you that you'll go out and make an effort to meet someone."

My mom doesn't get it at all. There's a reason I took a job in the middle of a mountain. Here, I can focus on my career with no distractions. There's a bar in Wild that I've been to with Kendra once when she dragged me out. But hanging out with strangers is not my thing.

"Put on a short skirt, sweetheart. Don't be afraid of those thighs you inherited from me. Some men love chunky girls. Look at your dad!"

She cackles like we've shared a secret, and my belly churns as I try not to think about my dad checking out my mom's thighs. Never mind the reference to my short stumpy legs. I'm immune to Mom's thoughtless comments by now.

When I'm not experimenting with new dessert recipes or thinking about new dessert recipes, I'm watching cooking shows and, on my days off, visiting every restaurant and cafe in the area to see what they've got on the menu. I may be shy, but I'm focused and determined. And I will not promise my mom that I'll go to a bar to look for men.

"I'm not going out to a bar, Mom."

"Oh honey…"

There's disappointment in her voice and she takes a deep breath, but before she can start the next lecture, I jump in.

"I already met someone."

I clamp my mouth shut as soon as I say the words. There's silence on the other end of the line.

"Say that again?"

"I…uh… met someone." I swallow hard, hoping she doesn't hear the lie in my voice.

"You've met a boy?"

"Ya-ha." My palms start to sweat. I've never been a good liar, and Mom is suspicious as hell.

"Are you going steady? Is he your boyfriend?"

My eyes go to Arlo leaning casually against the bar, a smile peeping out from his thick beard. "Yup. I got me a boyfriend."

"Oh MeMe. That's fantastic," my mother gushes. I wish she'd been this happy when I told her I got into culinary school or when I won the creative dessert award.

"What's he look like? Is he hunky?"

"Umm…" My gazes slides over Arlo, and I take a step closer to the door so I can see all of him through the small round window. His head is tilted back in a laugh, the deep rumble of his chuckle reaching me through the kitchen door and doing weird things to my belly.

"Um, he's tall and he's got a beard."

"A beard!" Mom exclaims. "I guess that's what you young folk are all into. But I wouldn't have looked twice at your father if he had a beard. What's his name."

"Arl..." I start to say and snap my mouth shut just in time. My fantasy almost got away from me, but I'm not giving out Arlo's name to my mother. She'd probably look him up online.

"What's that honey?"

"Allan." I wince.

"Allan? Not a very romantic name, but you can't help that. Where did you meet him?"

"Umm..." My brain freezes and I regret even starting this lie, but I'm in too deep to back out now. The best lies have a grain of truth, so I decide to stick to some semblance of realness. Besides, she'll never know. "He works at the restaurant."

"He's not a chef, is he? Unsociable hours. It'll hard when you have a family."

"Mom..."

"Oh, I know, honey, I'm just so excited. Thinking about my grandbabies. Jim!"

She calls out to my dad, making me wince and

wondering if I've just given her more fuel for the grandbaby pressure.

"Jim! MeMe's got a boyfriend!"

Dad mumbles something in the background. I don't know how my softspoken dad puts up with my mother. I've never met two such different people. Mom's loud and talks non-stop, while Dad's quiet and observant. I know which one I take after.

"We'll come visit this weekend and meet Allan."

Wait, what?

My attention snaps back to my mother. "You don't have to do that."

"Of course we do. My little girl's got her first boyfriend. We have to meet this Allan and see if he's good enough for you."

Oh shit.

My palms sweat, and panic sets in.

"Um, we're both working this weekend. Double shifts."

"That's alright, honey. We'll look around the mountains. We've been meaning to visit and see the place. There's some good shopping in Hope, I hear. Hey, does Allan fish? Should Dad bring his rod?"

Oh my god, this got out of control real fast. My palm goes to my forehead as I try to backtrack.

"Um, I don't know. Please don't come. It's too soon…"

But as usual Mom barrels over me.

"We've been meaning to come and check out the Wild Taste Restaurant. Dad's worried that it's run by a MC."

"But…" I try to protest that the Wild Riders are ex-military and not into anything sketchy, but Mom cuts me off.

"Oh, I know what you're going to say, but your dad wants to check it out for himself. See what the club that employs you is all about."

I stride to the kitchen door and peer out through the round window. Arlo sees me and holds up the last strawberry.

"It's good," he mouths, and my stomach does a little flip.

"I gotta go," says Mom. "We'll see you Friday, MeMe. You and Allan."

I press my head against the door and close my eyes.

What have I done?

To keep reading visit:
mybook.to/WRMCWildCurves

BOOKS AND SERIES BY SADIE KING

Wild Heart Mountain

Military Heroes

Wild Riders MC

Mountain Heroes

Temptation

A Runaway Bride for Christmas

A Secret Baby for Christmas

Knocked Up

Sunset Coast

Underground Crows MC

Sunset Security

Men of the Sea

Love and Obsession - The Cod Cove Trilogy

His Christmas Obsession

For a full list of Sadie King's books check out her website

www.authorsadieking.com

ABOUT THE AUTHOR

Sadie King is a USA Today Best Selling Author of contemporary romance novellas.

She lives in New Zealand with her ex-military husband and raucous young son.

When she's not writing she loves catching waves with her son, running along the beach, and drinking good wine with a book in hand.

Keep in touch when you sign up for her newsletter. You'll snag yourself a free short romance and access to all the bonus content!

authorsadieking.com/bonus-scenes

Printed in Great Britain
by Amazon

51980709R00076